THE TERRORS OF ROCK AND ROLL

4

I opened a door and stepped inside. Or rather, I stepped down. I gasped. Hissing rose around me like the hiss of steam. I screamed. The floor slithered beneath my shoes as though it were alive. I reached out towards the wall to get my balance, but I had already moved too far from the wall. I teetered on the balls of my feet, trying not to fall over. Something slippery tried to wriggle up my trouser leg. I looked down, my eyes gradually adjusting to the darkness. The sunken floor was covered with a writhing mass of snakes.

Susan Smith

SAMANTHA SLADE

THE TERRORS OF ROCK AND ROLL

4

Hippo Books
Scholastic Publications Limited
London

Scholastic Publications Ltd.,
10 Earlham Street, London WC2H 9RX, UK

Scholastic Inc.,
730 Broadway, New York, NY 10003, USA

Scholastic Tab Publications Ltd.,
123 Newkirk Road, Richmond Hill,
Ontario L4C 3G5, Canada

Ashton Scholastic Pty. Ltd.,
P O Box 579, Gosford, New South Wales,
Australia

Ashton Scholastic Ltd.,
165 Marua Road, Panmure, Auckland 6,
New Zealand

First published by
Pocket Books, a division of
Simon & Schuster Inc., USA, 1987

This edition published by Scholastic Publications Ltd., 1989

ISBN 0 590 76068 8

**For my sister Lesley,
with love**

Chapter 1

"SAMANTHA, LOOK AT that band!" cried Lupi, one of the children I babysit.

Lupi Brown, her brother Drake, and I had just come out of the sporting goods shop. I had bought ping-pong bats, a net, and some balls so I could teach them how to play ping-pong. I glanced across the Plainview Shopping Mall, trying to see where the squawky electronic sounds were coming from. Next to the ice-cream shop we could see a band warming up. All the band members were teenagers, clad in blue jeans and matching yellow T-shirts that read "Yellow Jackets".

Out of curiosity we walked over to listen to them. I noticed a poster advertising a "Battle of the Bands" contest propped up in front of the small stage.

"They're probably going to enter the 'Battle of the Bands'," suggested Lupi, an avid TV watcher. Then she clutched her hand over her heart. "I'd just love to be in a band."

Lupi already looked like a miniature rock star with her mane of wild blond hair and hypnotic blue eyes. To complete the image, she had taken to wearing boots and fringed shirts lately.

"Me, too," said Drake, pushing his thick dark hair away from his eyes. "I want to make a video for TV."

Drake, a mad scientist in his spare time, was eight years old, and both he and Lupi were very serious. Just by looking at them, no one would ever guess the two kids were really monsters.

The first line of the poster caught my eye:

$500 PRIZE
FOR THE BEST BAND IN THE STATE!
FILL IN YOUR ENTRY FORM TODAY
FOR THE STATEWIDE BATTLE OF
THE BANDS

If you have a band or any musical talent at all, sign up today. And remember, winning isn't everything in this contest. Bands are seen by local DJs and talent scouts, and yours could be one of them. You could be a star! Entries must be received no later than March 1. For contestants between 8 and 18 years of age.

BE A STAR!

"Can we watch, Samantha?" Drake wanted to know.

I had one more stop to make before we could go home, so I thought watching the band might keep the kids occupied until I was finished.

"Okay, but just stay here," I instructed them. "I'm going to shop for Iris' birthday present in Macy's," I said, pointing to the department store. "I'll come and get you when I'm finished."

"Okay," they chorused, already running to join the crowd around the band.

I felt a little nervous about leaving Lupi and Drake alone in a public place. They were capable of almost anything and I don't mean that in the ordinary sense. They were pretty much superhuman.

The town we live in, Plainview, is about as plain as it sounds. People like the Browns stand out here. When I first started babysitting for the kids, my life immediately changed from boring to ultra-exciting. I have to say that sometimes it's been too exciting.

For example, in the sporting goods shop, Lupi had discovered some baseball mitts and balanced a stack of them on her head. "What do you do with these, Samantha?" she asked me.

Well, of course, everyone in America knows what you do with them. I felt as if all the other customers were watching us. "Lupi, put those down," I pleaded. "I'll tell you all about them later."

Once the kids had brought Lupi's pet bat into the grocery shop owned by my friend Tommy's father, and it had caused a riot. We got kicked out, leaving the shop in ruins. But there is much, much more.

I decided to forget about the Browns while I went down the escalator to the junior department. I wandered around, looking at clothes and jewellery, and finally decided on an orange tie-dyed T-shirt. It was brightly coloured and seemed to suit Iris. She had been telling me for weeks that she wanted to be immensely important, and she had started to stock her wardrobe with more noticeable clothes.

I paid for the shirt, decided to wrap it at home, and walked out of the shop. By the time I reached the centre of the mall, I knew something had changed. I got this funny feeling in the pit of my stomach — a feeling I often got when Lupi and Drake were around.

I looked over at the platform where the Yellow Jackets had been playing. The crowd had grown in size, gathering tightly around the stage. Whoops and claps rose from the group. Then a strange, eerie birdlike note rose from the stage. I could see some of the band members, hands shoved in pockets, standing around in the crowd. I guessed that maybe another band had taken over.

As I moved closer, I saw that indeed somebody *had* taken over. The top of Lupi's shaggy blond head bobbed above the other heads. When I jumped up and down to peer above the crowd, I caught a glimpse of the two kids on the makeshift wooden platform, singing. I pushed towards the front of the crowd to get a better look at them.

Sure enough, Lupi held the microphone in her hand, singing a song I recognized but had never heard sung quite that way before. She made it sound wild and warbly. And Drake was adding all kinds of chatters, shrieks, and trills to her rhythm.

Suddenly Drake pulled some little stones and a tiny bottle out of his pocket and laid them down in front of him on the stage. He uncorked the bottle and sprinkled some yellow dust over the stones.

In the blink of an eye the stones changed into coins! Bright silver coins — quarters, half-dollars and dimes! The crowd gasped in surprise, pressing forward to get a closer look.

"Did you see that?" they exclaimed.

An excited murmur travelled through the audience as Drake repeated the procedure. Some people picked up a handful of the coins to see whether they were real.

The band members who accompanied Lupi and Drake lost their places in the music as they watched the kids' performance. Drake and Lupi, apparently not noticing, just kept right on singing. Lupi pranced across the stage, accidently kicking the bag of ping-pong balls. The balls scattered off the stage, bouncing down into the audience. People stooped to pick up the balls and put them back on the stage. The kids seemed totally unruffled by this; Drake simply picked up a few balls and started to juggle them, bouncing them off the top of Lupi's head. Then Lupi got out the ping-pong net and wrapped it around her head. She began to bare her teeth and behave like a caged animal, which, in a way, she was.

I stopped scrounging around on the floor for the runaway ping-pong balls and watched Lupi closely. It always made me nervous when she acted like that because you never knew with

Lupi. She had a very strange quality — she was a real werewolf. I wanted to see if her eyes were turning yellow.

The crowd broke into applause. Drake started to hand out coins and the audience passed them around for examination.

"No doubt about it," somebody said. "It's the real stuff."

The music started up again, weaving harmoniously around everyone. The crowd listened intently, as though struck by some kind of magic.

At last the band stopped playing and Lupi's and Drake's voices faded into whispers. The crowd pressed closer, full of questions.

"How did you do that — with the stones?" somebody asked.

"It's a potion," Drake replied.

"A potion? How extraordinary!"

"A little too extraordinary if you ask me," one of the band members complained. "I'm sure it's just a cheap trick from the magic shop."

"It didn't come from the magic shop," Lupi growled, her voice growing deeper.

"What a sensation!"

I started to get really nervous. All this attention could go to the kids' heads. And I didn't like their telling people about their potions and magic — even though most people didn't really believe it even when they saw it with their own eyes. Speaking of eyes, Lupi's eyes had changed from clear blue to yellow — not a good sign at all.

"Are you going to be on TV?" somebody else asked.

"Yeah, they can be the world's greatest band crashers," a voice grumbled behind me.

I turned around to see who had spoken. It was one of the displaced band members.

"I'm sure they didn't mean any harm," I told him. "They're just kids having a good time."

"Yeah, that's what we thought, too. So we let them sing."

"Don't worry," I said, motioning to Lupi and Drake. "I'm sure they won't bother you again. Thanks for letting them have a chance."

The band member sighed. "Maybe if I practise enough, I'll learn to make money, too, — ha-ha."

Lupi ran over to me, still covered in the ping-pong net.

"You can take that off now," I told her.

"I like it on," she replied.

"Maybe we should leave it on," Drake suggested. "She might need it."

I grimaced. "Okay, if you say so. But I think we'd better leave. People are getting too curious about you."

We gathered up our stuff and started to hurry out of the mall. But as we moved away from the crowd, Lupi got her ping-pong net hooked onto a man's umbrella. I was so preoccupied with making a fast getaway that I only glanced at his face, forming a fleeting impression of dark glasses, short, with thin blond hair.

"Oh, excuse us," I said in a rush, struggling to untangle the net from the umbrella. The stranger's fingers on the umbrella and net seemed to move unbelievably slowly. I fidgeted impatiently until Lupi freed herself. Then she growled and began pawing at the net as though she wanted to free herself from it too.

The stranger stared at her with interest. I suddenly noticed another man wearing a plaid suit and golf shoes standing behind him, watching this whole scene carefully. He held several posters under his arm, but all I could see of the posters was "Vote for—".

"How did you do that money trick, kid?" the man in the plaid suit asked excitedly.

"It's not a trick," Drake explained. "It's a potion."

The man laughed. "It looked pretty real — very impressive. But it had to be a trick."

"No, it's not," Drake insisted. "I invented a potion that turns things into money."

Both men laughed, but they looked very curious.

"Come on, we have to get going," I interrupted, quickly leading Lupi and Drake away.

I didn't think any more about the two men because as soon as we got outside, I became conscious of Lupi's hand in mine. Just as we got to the pavement, I started to notice how different her hand felt. I glanced down to get a better look at it.

It had become furry.

Then I stared into her face. She had sprouted a few whiskers, and when she grinned at me, I saw that her teeth had grown yellow and sharp. I glanced around wildly to see if anyone had noticed her, but the few scattered shoppers in the car park didn't seem to be looking at us.

"Look at her, Drake!" I cried. "We have to

get out of here — fast."

"We can take a bus," he suggested mildly.

"No, we can't. She's changing too fast." I could just imagine people seeing a werewolf in their midst and scrambling to get out of the bus. "Let's go through the canyon. We shouldn't run into many people there at this time of year."

Of course, we'd been through this before, with Lupi's changing into a werewolf, but she had never done it in public. She had always been either a werewolf when everyone first saw her or just a normal kid. The in-between Lupi was much scarier for me because I felt as if I were watching a horror show. And the worst part of it was seeing it happen to my friend.

As we ran towards the canyon, the rest of the changes took place. Lupi trailed her newly formed claws along the slats of a picket fence, leaving jagged marks in the paint. The animal contours of her face had deepened, and big tufts of fur appeared in place of her eyebrows.

"Lupi, how are you feeling?" I asked her.

She growled at me. "Big and furry."

I tried to imagine what that might feel like. By the time we reached the canyon, Lupi's face had hardened into the sharp and definite look of an animal. She ran beside us on all fours.

Some kids playing hopscotch on the pavement pointed at Lupi and asked, "What is that? Is it a dog?"

"It's a werewolf, silly. Haven't you ever seen a werewolf before?" another one cried. He obviously thought it was someone dressed up in a costume.

In the canyon birds shrieked and flew away as

we passed. We could hear squirrels and other small animals scattering in fright. We created quite a stir.

Finally we emerged from the canyon near the Browns' house.

Lupi's gaze swept up and down the quiet street. "I'm hungry," she growled.

"What do we do with her now?" I asked Drake. "Throw her a piece of raw meat?"

"We have some tasty fish eyelids at our house," Drake suggested. "Lupi loves those."

At the mention of the food Lupi let out a loud growl and loped down the pavement in front of us. Drake and I struggled to keep up with her, but Lupi was extra strong and fast as a werewolf.

Instead of running straight home, she galloped past the house — towards a couple who leaned up against a car, talking.

"Sarah, what is that? Is that what I think it is?" the man asked.

"Yes, and it's not even Halloween, George," exclaimed the woman called Sarah.

Lupi drew dangerously close to them, growling menacingly. The couple cringed in fright.

Just as Lupi raised her claws, Drake and I caught up with her and grabbed her arms, one of us on each side. Tugging and pulling, we hauled her away from the couple.

"Lupi, the joke's gone far enough," I said soothingly. "You really scared those people."

"Yes, you certainly did," agreed the man named George. "That's a really authentic outfit."

"Thank you," Lupi growled deeply.

"Even down to the claws," the woman added, reaching out to examine them.

"Careful," I warned. The woman stared at me curiously.

Lupi's whole furry body stiffened, resisting us. But with great effort we turned her around and marched her, or dragged her, back home.

There was no telling what she might do in this state, so I felt really relieved when we finally got her behind closed doors.

Once inside the Browns' house, I sank into the nearest chair in the dark living room. I looked around the curious room filled with all sorts of odd things: a tank of live, flesh-eating piranhas, a shrunken head on the mantelpiece, a floor-to-ceiling spider web in one corner. The place had all the atmosphere of a haunted house. In fact, when I first visited the house, I thought the family had decorated specially for Halloween. At that time, of course, I had no idea I'd be babysitting for a family of monsters.

I had just about relaxed when something furry sprang into my lap. I gasped, but it was only Claws, the Browns' black cat. She dropped something warm into my lap and leapt away. I looked down and saw a freshly dead mouse staring vacantly back at me.

I sighed and shook my head.

Chapter 2

ON FRIDAY NIGHT I stopped my bike at the drive-up box at Burger Headquarters and ordered my food.

"I want a burger, small fries, and a chocolate milkshake." I spoke in a funny voice.

A loud squawk followed by a staticky voice came from the box. "*Huhhmmmmm.*"

"I can't understand you!" I cried in exasperation.

"*Hhmmhuhuh,*" the voice repeated.

"Listen, I can't understand you, but this is what I want," I said, and I repeated my order.

"A burger, small fries, and a chocolate shake," the voice crackled from the box, but at least this time I could understand what she was saying. And I knew the voice belonged to my best friend, Iris Martin. "Anything else?"

"Do you have any chocolate pies?"

"We don't sell chocolate pies."

"How about roast beef sandwiches?"

"We don't have any roast beef sandwiches," Iris screeched into the microphone. "Is there *anything else?*"

I knew she would kill me if I kept it up, so I

said, "No, that's all. But what did I order?"

"Fries, burger, and chocolate shake," she replied with a crackly sigh.

"Leave off the onions, okay?"

"Okay."

On my bicycle, I followed the car in front of me. I saw Iris stick her head out of the drive-up window and hand the customer in front of me a bag of food. Then it was my turn.

I grinned as I rode up to the window and peered in at her.

"You should tell them to fix that speaker," I said with a smile.

"Sam!" she cried, wrinkling her freckled nose. "I should've known it was you. Especially when you said leave off the onions."

I took my bag of food and laughed. "A lot of people say that. It's really not all that original."

"No, but after the other stuff — boy, am I tired of the practical jokers," she complained.

"Even me?" I asked.

Before she could answer, the car behind me started honking. Iris motioned for me to come inside. I parked my bike and went into the restaurant.

She finished serving her next customer and took her break. We sat down together and I ate my food while she talked.

She pushed a strand of sandy hair under her white cap and bit into one of my fries.

"This job is driving me nuts, Sam," she whispered. "It's Friday night, and every joker in the world is out, including you."

I giggled.

"It's not the least bit funny, I'd rather be at

the pictures, and here I am watching other people get ready to go to the pictures," she complained. "I'm tired of smelling like a french fry, and I'm sick of saying the same old words: 'Burger, shake, and fries.' There's no variation. I'm tired of those little chicken pieces that look like chicken thumbs."

"Chicken thumbs!" I exclaimed. "You know, they really do look like chicken thumbs — or like you'd imagine them if chickens really did have thumbs, that is."

"Yeah, well, people love them," Iris told me. "They don't care what part of the chicken they come from."

"So why don't you quit?" I suggested.

"This is the first real job I've ever had and I need the money," she replied. "But I'm going to look for something else. My mother said she might be able to get me a job with her foot doctor."

"What would you do?" I asked.

"I don't know yet. I sure don't want to touch anybody's feet," she shuddered.

"Maybe you wouldn't have to have any sort of human contact," I reassured her. "Why don't we go to the pictures when you're all done here?"

"I don't get off until ten o'clock," she moaned. "Maybe tomorrow."

"Okay. But you know, Iris, a lot of really talented people have had crummy, mindless jobs in their lifetimes."

"Oh, really?" Iris blinked at me.

"Yes. Charles Dickens, John Steinbeck . . . "

"Well, I think I could stand having a

crummy job if I had the talent those guys did," Iris said.

"You *do* have talent," I insisted. "Remember when you played the spoons for the second-grade talent show? And you were in a choral group."

Iris and I had gone through school together; there wasn't much we didn't know about each other. And what one of us forgot the other remembered, so between us we were like an archive of our own history.

"Oh, yeah," she replied thoughtfully. "What I really want to do is a comedy routine, but I don't think I'm that funny."

"I think you're funny," I said loyally.

"Great. So I have an audience of one — my loyal friend." She laughed.

"Everybody loved you as a piece of Swiss cheese," I reminded her, recalling Iris' prize-winning Halloween costume.

"You can't go through life as a piece of Swiss cheese. After a while it isn't funny anymore." She sighed. "I keep thinking of your giving that frog speech," Iris went on. "Nothing can top that for humour."

"I only wish it had won me the election," I grumbled. I had run for class president, but lost the election — even after that speech. Although I'd got over over losing, I still had this notion that I wanted to do something wonderful and important.

"Yeah, but you *almost* won, Sam," she reminded me.

"Well, that was because of our combined efforts," I told her encouragingly, because without Iris' help, I could never have pulled off the whole thing. "I think up something, and then you come up with the rest of the ideas. You're good at that."

"I am, aren't I?" She smiled.

I was glad she was starting to see herself in a different light. That was the great thing about Iris and me. When one of us didn't feel too hot about herself, the other one was always there to boost her spirits. It was as if we were Siamese twins or something. We knew all of each other's good and bad points, and we knew how to make the most of each of them.

"Thanks for the pep talk." Iris stood up from the table. "I feel better now. Ready to face another fifty million orders."

"That's great, becuase look who's here." I pointed towards the door at Monica Hammond, class president and my rival in the election. Monica was also the most popular girl in the third form at Davis Junior High.

"Oh, make my day," muttered Iris, wrinkling her freckled nose in distaste.

Monica glided over to us, grinning. "Hi, Iris, hi, Samantha," she oozed. "You work here now, Iris?"

She said it as though she'd just found Iris making mud pies.

Iris laughed. "No, I just thought I'd try on the uniform for size."

"It's so greasy," Monica said. "You must have to wash your hair every night."

"Actually, I love the smell of fries," answered Iris, winking at me.

"Did you guys hear about the Battle of the

Bands yet?" Monica asked, tossing her hair over her shoulder.

"Uh, no," Iris replied.

"Oh, yeah," I said. Iris looked at me, and I explained. "It's a contest for kids under eighteen. The prize is five hundred dollars for the winning band. You have to tour all over the state, playing in different places."

"And I'm entering it," Monica announced proudly.

Iris turned to me. "Are you thinking what I'm thinking?"

"Yes, but we don't have a band," I reminded her.

"I can play spoons," said Iris, laughing.

"Spoons?" Monica questioned. I explained, and she grimaced.

"Sounds interesting." She tossed her head back. "I've already got a band. We've been rehearsing."

"You do?" Iris and I chorused.

"Yes. Some really wonderful people," Monica gushed. The word "wonderful" came out with all the emphasis, as if she were a film star or something.

"I'd like to have a band," Iris mused.

"Well, good luck," said Monica.

"Did I hear you say 'band'?" a voice spoke up behind me.

I turned around. The voice belonged to Tommy Deere, the boy I'm crazy about. Tommy is also a terrific friend, and we've been through a lot together. He even knows a few of the secret, crazy things about the Brown family that I haven't shared with anyone else, not even

Iris.

"Yes, Monica was telling us about her band for the Battle of the Bands contest," I replied.

Iris moved back behind the counter.

Monica batted her eyelashes at Tommy, who sort of blinked in confusion. What a creep! Flirting with Tommy, right in front of my eyes!

Then she looked up at the menu and sighed, "I guess I'll have the salad bar."

"To stay or to go?" asked Iris.

"To go." Monica paid for her food and Iris issued her a bowl for her salad.

Monica turned abuptly so that her long hair swung over her shoulders. "Well, see you in class."

After she had gone, Iris said, "I really want to be in a band."

"Yeah, me too," Tommy agreed. "Five hundred dollars is a great prize, and besides, it would be alot of fun."

"Sam plays the piano and I play spoons," Iris informed him.

"Spoons?" Tommy laughed. "Well, I play guitar. Why don't we get together and practise and see how we sound?"

"I think we'll need more people to make a band. But maybe I know some people . . . " I said, thinking of Lupi's and Drake's performance in the mall. I didn't want to volunteer them, though. As much as I loved them, I thought having them in our band would be a disaster.

The next day, Saturday, Iris and I went to the pictures. Afterwards we ate at a pizza place, because Iris couldn't stand eating hamburgers anymore. For a while she had been into health foods, and then she stopped — but working at Burger Headquarters was making her change again.

Then we bought some blond hair dye and dyed Iris' hair. It turned out sort of brassy. I had to babysit at five, so we spent the rest of the afternoon playing with the clear plastic gloves that came with the hair dye. We filled them with water and threw them at each other. We drew faces on them. Finally we arranged them on Iris' doorknob so that they looked like plastic hands.

At five o'clock I hurried to the Browns' house to babysit. It was nearly dark when I ran up the steps to their front porch. I pressed the doorbell and was suddenly shocked out of my skin. Instead of the doorbell, an ear-shattering alarm blasted throughout the house.

Nobody rushed to answer the door. Silence followed the alarm itself, a silence that was even more alarming than the alarm itself. I vaguely remembered Lupi's telling me she'd found an alarm in an auto parts store, but I sure didn't expect her to use it this way.

Someone opened the door a crack and with a lightning-fast motion, reached an arm out, grabbed the front of my jacket, and roughly yanked me inside.

The bag of biscuits I was carrying fell to the ground. In the dark hallway I found myself pressed up against a creature whose breath was foul and dead and made me want to retch. I thought it must be Uncle Tompkins, the mummy. But when I looked up, I saw grey stringy hair clumped around the pinched-in face of a woman whose eyes bored into mine like hot coals.

I gasped.

"*Shhh!*" hissed the creature. "You look so-o-o juicy."

"N-not really," I stammered. "I'm all skin and bones."

"Cousin!" Lupi called.

You wouldn't believe how glad I was that she had come to rescue me.

She marched up to her cousin. "Let go of Samantha," she ordered. "You can't bite her. She's our friend."

"Friend, schmend," Cousin cried. "She has a heart, doesn't she?"

"Of course she does, but you're supposed to be teaching us music," Lupi reminded her.

So this was Cousin Antonia, the musical one.

Lupi tugged on my sleeve. "Come on, Samantha, we're all set up in my room."

I looked from her to her cousin. "Uh, Lupi. Can you tell her to let go of me, please?"

Lupi whirled around. "Cousin Antonia, let go!" Cousin Antonia wagged her head, refusing to give up her hold on me until Lupi pulled her clawlike hands off me. Her fingers brushed against my cheek, giving me a chill. Her skin felt like wet dish towels.

"So nice of you to bring new blood into the house." Cousin Antonia grinned, revealing pointed, fanglike teeth.

I gasped. She looked like a . . .

"Cousin Antonia is a vampire," explained Lupi, as we walked through the house and upstairs. "You have to watch her — if you have any veins, that is." She giggled, but I didn't think it was funny at all, and I told her so.

"It's okay for you, Lupi," I insisted. "You're used to her. But what if she bites me?"

"Samantha, you worry too much." Lupi laughed as she pulled me along. "I'll take care of you."

I wondered who was doing the babysitting — Lupi or me. She led me to her room, and I cringed as I passed through the doorway, which was laced with spiderwebs. Lupi offered me a place on the animal-skin rug, next to a big stuffed bear who sat on a spike-seated chair.

Antonia settled down in front of us on the bed. She looked like a small heap of rags, her cape patched in a million places. She bowed her head and muttered a few words in some foreign language before raising her hands to the ceiling. She didn't do anything a normal music teacher would.

"First I will teach you all harmony so that you can get along in the music, and then I'll teach you where discord belongs," she explained.

"I didn't know discord belonged anywhere," I objected.

"It has its place in music," Antonia smiled patiently. "Without it, music is uninteresting."

With that, Antonia opened her big mouth and began to sing. The air whistled through the spaces in her pointy teeth and her voice warbled and stung my ears. Then it turned into something vibrating and unusual.

A little girl with a short, uneven haircut burst

into the room. She was Lupi's and Drake's small cousin, Kimmie, a telekinetic. She joined right in, jumping up and down to the rhythm. Then she started clapping her hands together and doing somersaults. When Kimmie got very excited like this, she made objects move around just by thinking about them. Suddenly sheets of music floated off the the music stand and fluttered around the room, sticking to the walls and corners. When I reached down to pick them up, the parchment crumbled in my hands. Wow, this music must be hundreds of years old, I thought. Maybe it should be in a museum instead of flying around the bedroom.

Then Kimmie must have focused on the music stand, because it flew straight into the fireplace just as Antonia hit her highest note, which ran through me like a spear.

The glass windowpanes started to shake as Antonia held that awful note. I had a sudden urge to put my hands over my ears, but I didn't want to look rude. Antonia went on and on. I couldn't stand it. If she taught Lupi to sing like that, we'd all go completely crazy.

Finally she stopped and wrung her hands. "We must all sing together now," she announced. She made a strange twisting gesture with her arm, and Lupi started to sing a song I had never heard before.

"Samantha, join in, please," Antonia ordered.

"I'm not a singer," I protested, but one scorching look from Antonia had me singing anyway.

Suddenly we heard a loud banging at the

front door.

We all stopped singing and looked at one another. "I'll get it," I offered.

I ran downstairs and opened the door, but I couldn't find anybody there. Laughter suddenly bubbled up behind me, and I turned sharply.

"You didn't need to open the door. I can move right through it," a voice informed me, and then a ghostly, humanlike form materialized.

"Samantha, it's just Lucy — one of the ghosts," said Drake as he came up behind me. "Say hello to her quickly though. She'll probably want to go straight down to the basement because Antonia is here."

"Antonia?" the ghost shrieked in a breathy sort of way. Half of her body disappeared through the wall.

"Did someone call my name?" Antonia bellowed, her voice cutting the air like a knife.

Lucy shrieked again. Antonia sniffed the air. "Ah, a blasted ghost. I can't stand them. *Ahhh*!" She ran towards the ghost, arms outstretched, ready to attack. Drake and I watched as the ghost darted away from the wall and vanished through the closed trapdoor that led to the basement.

"Drat! You spoiled all my fun, Drake," Antonia pouted. She let out a loud, bloodcurdling note and flounced away.

"Why does she want to chase ghosts?" I asked. "They don't even have blood."

"They make her mad. And she loves to scare them," explained Drake. "She calls them bloodless nothings."

"But they're already . . . dead. They've got nothing left to lose."

"I know. But most of them are very timid and she threatens to take away their spirits. Of course, she can't really do it, but the ghosts don't know that." Then he started back down the hall. "Come on. Let's go sing."

Reluctantly, I followed Drake back to Lupi's room. Spending time in the company of a vampire was not exactly my idea of fun.

Chapter 3

ON MONDAY MORNING Iris and I were standing at our locker when Tommy approached us.

"Do you both want to come over this afternoon and hear me play guitar?" he asked.

"Oh, sure," I answered. "That would be great."

"That way we can find out how compatible we are," Tommy suggested. "We have a piano, too."

"Great! And we can find out what songs to play in the contest." I realized that that sounded like I had already decided we'd be compatible, so I opened my mouth to say something else.

But Tommy had already started to walk away. "I'll pick you guys up at your locker after school." He grinned and waved at us.

I whirled around, turning to Iris. "Did you hear that?"

She frowned. "Of course I heard, Sam. I'm not deaf."

"Right." I was so excited I could barely talk. I couldn't eat lunch. I even dropped yogurt down the front of my shirt, which stained in a big pear shape.

"Maybe I can go home and change after school," I told Iris as we left the cafeteria.

"You won't have time," she insisted. "You'll have to go like that."

I suppose I could have lived with it, until Monica eyeballed my stain and cried, "*Euww*, Samantha, what did you spill on yourself?"

"I barfed on myself, Monica," I said, just to be gross.

She laughed. I was glad she found it so funny, because I didn't think it was funny at all.

Tommy met us right after school and we all walked to his house. His father, whom I'd met before at his grocery shop, welcomed us inside. Unfortunately he remembered me.

"You're the girl who babysits the Brown kids. Didn't I kick you out of my shop once?" he asked jovially.

"Dad," warned Tommy, glancing at me helplessly.

"Uh, yes, that was me," I mumbled, turning twenty shades of red.

"I hear that's a pretty wild family," Mr Deere went on, laughing.

"That's what they say," I replied noncommittally. I suppose the Browns had been seen around in their various forms of oddness, and they were hard not to notice.

"What some people won't do for attention," Mr Deere commented.

"We're starting a band, Dad," Tommy interrupted.

"Oh, great. Well, nice to see you again,

Samantha," Mr Deere said.

"You, too," I told him.

"It was nice meeting you, too, Iris," Mr Deere added.

"Thanks, Mr Deere," Iris, suppressing a giggle.

We followed Tommy into the den, a room decorated with couches and lots of videos and computer equipment. Books lined the walls.

"Are you a computer person?" I asked.

"Yeah." He laughed. "A total nerd." Then he picked up his guitar and strummed softly.

"Play something," I urged.

"Yeah," Iris chimed in, perching herself on the arm of a couch.

Tommy sat down on a swivel chair and started playing. I thought he was great slicing cold meat, but he was even better playing the guitar. His hands moved over the strings fluidly, and the notes that came forth tumbled over each other with enthusiasm. He looked as if he enjoyed what he was doing, and I loved the way he looked when he was concentrating.

Then he started to sing a popular song we all knew — but it sounded different the way he sang it.

"Oh, there is some place to go . . . that only I know, and there's someone that I see . . . who is waiting there for me . . . "

I closed my eyes and wondered if he was talking about me. Well, I knew he couldn't really be talking about me because somebody else had written that song a long time before Tommy and I knew each other. But I decided that Tommy might be *thinking* about me while he was singing. That was sort of possible. But I still wasn't sure if Tommy knew how I felt about him. When I had run for president, he had snitched a photograph of me off one of my campaign posters, which made me think he must like me, too.

He stopped playing.

"That was great!" cried Iris, clapping.

I joined in. "Bravo! You're really good."

"Let's play something together. Do you know 'Give Me Your Wallet'?" Tommy asked.

"No, but I'll improvise," I offered. I sat down at the piano, and Tommy went to the kitchen to get spoons for Iris.

Then we started.

"A one, and a two, and a . . . " Tommy started the song, I came in next, and then Iris. "Give me your wallet, hand it over right now. I'll give you a wild time, I'll show you how."

After we had played a few songs together, we decided to take a break.

"We're great!" exclaimed Tommy. "I taped us just so we could hear how we sound together."

We listened to ourselves on tape and were impressed.

"We'll still need other people," Tommy said thoughtfully. "Let's hold some auditions this week to try to find people for the group. We can have the auditions here — no problem."

After we left Tommy's, Iris told me, "You know, Sam, I'm really suprised. I mean, I thought all Tommy Deere could do was cut up bologna. Boy, was I wrong."

I laughed. "Yeah, I used to think so, too, Iris.

Except I always knew there was more to Tommy than what I saw."

"You always knew." Iris mimicked me, which she did well. "How come you always *know* so much? Do you read people's minds or something?"

"No, I just sensed it," I retorted. I couldn't tell her that I'd got to know Tommy really well when he had helped us hide Bubbles, the monster that the Brown family had imported to liven things up around their house. When Bubbles had become a nuisance living in the backyard, Tommy had helped us find her a new home in the woods.

"That's crazy, Sam, and you know it. You sound like some kind of a witch or something," Iris huffed as we walked down the street.

"No, I don't," I insisted. "You just don't understand anything, that's what's wrong with you."

We argued playfully until we got to her house. It was nearly dark and the leafless trees stuck out against the sky like claws. I still thought I was right and she was wrong. Iris is so practical that I think it's almost a fault. She would never believe in anything like reincarnation, for instance. And, she wouldn't know a witch if one came up and kissed her.

The kids who auditioned for our band on Thursday were not exactly what we had in mind. We decided not to choose any of them.

Earlier that day, Iris and I had been walking past the music room at school when we heard Monica rehearsing with her band. They had drums, guitars, a bass, and Monica could really sing. They called themselves The Spectaculars and they sounded great.

"Gee, if they're The Spectaculars, what does that make us?" Iris asked.

"It doesn't mean a thing, Iris," I said. "But what does mean something is that so far they have everything and we don't. We'll have to do something even more spectacular."

That night I went to the Browns'. Dr Brown, the children's mother, let me in.

"Samantha, darling, it's s-so nice to see you," she greeted me quickly. "The children have been waiting for you downstairs. They've found some of our old instruments and want to show them to you."

Dr Brown, dressed in a strange flowing gown of multicoloured strips of animal skin, took my hand and stepped ahead of me. I pulled back suddenly as she dropped through the floor.

"Samantha? Aren't you coming?" I heard her call as she fell to the basement.

"Uh, I'll be down in a minute," I replied, because I didn't want to travel by way of the trapdoor. Ever since they installed it, I've had to watch my step when I come in the house.

Carefully I walked down the steps to the basement. Below me I saw Lupi, Drake, and their parents huddled around a big chest, their faces lit by candlelight.

"Samantha, come here," cried Lupi. "We've found Uncle Tompkins' old Burmese jaws harp. It hasn't been played in ages, but it sounds wonderful."

She reached for my hand as I drew near,

handing me the jaws harp: a small piece of bamboo, notched at one end, with a tiny sliver of bamboo attached over the notch.

"What do you do with it?" I asked.

"You put it against your mouth. When you sing, the sliver of bamboo vibrates and makes this sound." She demonstrated for me; it sounded nice and kind of eerie.

"Now look at this." Drake handed me a bone with ridges along the side of it. He ran it along the side of a box, making a rippling sound.

"Can't we turn on some lights?" I asked. "I can't see."

"Oh, Samantha, of course." Mr Brown chuckled, smiling his toothy smile at me. "We forgot that you don't have our kind of vision."

He turned on a gas lamp in the corner and light flickered on the bare walls. Then I noticed the snake draped around Dr Brown's neck. When it flicked its fork tongue at me, I jumped about half a foot.

"Oh, don't be afraid, Samantha. Let me introduce you to Lawrence," she said formally.

"Nice to meet you, Lawrence." I felt relieved that snakes didn't have hands to shake. Lawrence gave me the creeps.

"This empty tortoise shell is also an instrument," Drake interrupted.

"Do you play stringed instruments, Samantha? Here's an exquisite lute," said Dr Brown, handing me an old stringed instrument, a little like a guitar, inlaid with abalone.

I shook my head. "No, I'm sorry, I don't play."

Dr Brown strummed dreamily on the lute for

a few minutes before she and Mr Brown said goodnight and left us alone downstairs.

Dr and Mr Brown were going to a meeting of the Monster Preservation Society. Mr Brown was the president of the Society. I don't really know how many monsters they have to preserve, or any of the details of their work, I only know that the members seem as strange as the Browns and they all wear monklike gowns.

I took the lute and ran my thumb over the two remaining strings. Its tone was interrupted by a scrabbling sound, just before a little furry creature scrambled out of the hole in the instrument's deep box and scurried up my arm. He paused for a minute, meeting my gaze with black, beady eyes. I gasped.

"A rat!" I shrieked, shaking my arm wildy to get it off.

The rat jumped off me, its nails making little scratching noises on the hard cement floor. It reminded me of the dead mouse that Claws had dropped in my lap.

"I wonder how many creatures make their homes in these musical instruments," Drake said solemnly.

"Not many, I hope." I shivered.

"Are you okay, Samantha?" Lupi asked.

"I'm just fine," I replied, but I wasn't fine at all. I was trying to forget the image of twitching whiskers and those round, black button eyes staring into mine.

"I think Antonia would be great in a music video," said Drake. "She's a wonderful musician and singer, and I haven't seen anyone like her on TV."

"I don't know, Drake." I shuddered. "I think Antonia may be too scary for most people."

"Come on upstairs," he urged. "I want to show you our clavichord."

"Oh, I'd love to see it." I eagerly followed the kids through the house.

They led me into a part of the house that I'd never entered before: up a circular staircase, through masses of tickly cobwebs, then along a dark corridor. Lupi lit the way with a candle, which made our shadows dance along the walls. At the end of the corridor stood a door with a big wooden bolt across it. Lupi leaned her body against the bolt and shoved it back. Then we all pushed against the door, huffing and puffing until it inched open.

Lupi squeezed through the doorway first, then Drake and I followed.

The room, full of sheet-shrouded furniture, was covered with a fine layer of dust. Drake pulled back the heavy curtains and sunlight streamed through the windows.

"How long has this room been closed up?" I asked.

"Since just after we moved in. Uncle Tompkins lived here for a while, before he moved into the backyard," Lupi explained.

The Browns liked to keep all their friends and family around after death in one form or another, and their dear uncle, a mummy, was just one example — not someone you would want to run into very often.

"Here it is," Lupi whispered. She flung back one of the shrouds to reveal an ancient keyboard instrument with short yellowed keys. I stepped up to it and ran my fingers along the ornate side of the instrument. Snakes and dragons had been carved into the wood.

"This is fantastic!" I cried. I sat down on the rickety bench and began to play.

But just as I started, a funny sound rose from inside the instrument where all the keys are connected. It sounded like somebody — or something — breathing.

When I stopped playing, the noise stopped.

"What's that noise?" I asked.

"The instrument, of course!" exclaimed Lupi, laughing at me.

"But there's another noise, Lupi. Listen." I played some more. The noise breathed in time to the music. When I stopped playing, it bubbled to a halt.

"It sounds — almost human," I gasped, shuddering.

"It's not human," Drake corrected me. "It's Muki. He lives inside the instrument. The clavichord wouldn't work without him."

"But that's crazy!" I exclaimed.

Suddenly a loud groan that made the whole instrument tremble filled the room.

"Samantha, you don't understand," explained Drake. "Muki is in charge of the instrument. He lives in it. If you want to play it, you have to get along with him."

My hand accidentally dropped onto the keyboard, making a loud, discordant sound. Muki moaned loudly, and I glared at Lupi and Drake.

Then I turned back to the instrument and

yelled, "Hey, are you all right in there?"

Muki made a grumbling sound.

"He's very sensitive. Music is his whole life," Lupi told me. She lifted the top of the instrument. "Come here, Samantha." She stuck her head inside the instrument so that her voice resonated. "Hi, Muki, I want you to meet Samantha."

Cautiously, I walked over to stand next to Lupi. I peered over the edge to look inside the instrument. There, lying across the inside workings of the instrument, was a hairless mammal. That's the best I can do for a body description — sort of like a Mexican hairless dog. But when it lifted its head, a pair of huge sorrowful eyes met mine.

A pain struck me in the heart. Something in me softened, and I smiled.

"Hi, Muki," I said quietly. I even stuck my hand inside as a gesture. "I'm Samantha."

Muki didn't take my hand, but he rubbed his hairless ears against the strings, which made the instrument purr and hum.

"That means he's happy to meet you," explained Lupi. "He hopes that you and he will make beautiful music together."

"How nice of him," I said. "I'm sure we will."

"He says he likes the way you play, but he'd prefer it if you didn't pound on the keys," she added. "It hurts."

"Oh, okay," I agreed. I had visions of the poor creature being smashed on the inside of the instrument — all because of my playing. "How long has he lived in there?"

"Always," Drake answered. "He came with instrument."

I laughed. "Buy a piano and get your own built-in monster. Great. Every home should have one."

"They don't live in modern instruments?" asked Lupi seriously.

"Not as far as I know," I replied. "I guess you don't get much for your money these days."

"How disappointing," she said.

"Instruments cost money?" Drake asked me.

"Of course."

"Then they must be like video cameras," he said. "I've been pricing them."

I often forget how ignorant the Browns are about money. They have no idea of the cost of things. Once Dr Brown had given me a hundred-dollar bill to buy hot dogs at the corner shop.

"Why don't you try playing again, Samantha?" suggested Drake.

I sighed. "Okay." I sat down on the bench and started to play. Muki hummed along with the music, which had a funny effect on me. Goose pimples rose on my arms. I shivered.

If you were to rate the Browns' monsters and relatives on a scale from one to ten for weirdness, a music monster would come in at about five. He wasn't all that strange. In fact, the more I played the clavichord, the more I liked the monster.

Chapter 4

ON FRIDAY, a school holiday, Iris, Tommy, and I decided to go to see a movie at the mall. As we were walking to the cinema, I glanced over at the entrance to Macy's and saw a band playing.

"Hey, it must be somebody advertising for the Battle of the Bands," said Iris.

As we dew closer, I recognized the faces beneath the odd makeup and eighteenth-century clothing: Lupi and Drake. Dr and Mr Brown stood near the stage, clapping. But they didn't clap like other people — they clapped their hands against their cheeks.

"Hey, come on, let's go watch," Tommy said eagerly.

"We'll miss the movie," I warned.

"So, we'll see the next showing," he insisted.

"Yeah, come on, Sam," Iris urged. "Look at the crowd. They must be pretty good."

I knew that as soon as my friends saw Lupi and Drake, they would want them in our band. And I was right.

The two children almost looked like Dickens characters, Drake in a raggedy black suit and Lupi in a black Victorian dress with lots of lace.

These outfits, the sort of clothes that kids of today wouldn't be caught dead wearing, probably came from their vast collection of antique clothes. Together they sang a song called "The Scare Song", and when he wasn't singing, Drake played a single note by blowing into a conch shell.

"Samantha, why didn't you tell us they were so good?" Tommy wanted to know.

"Yeah, Sam." Iris stared at me, hands on her hips.

"I thought of it, but then I figured we'd want somebody older," I explained.

"You were probably right about that," Iris admitted. She threaded her way through the crowd to get a better look. One of the backup band members was giving out handbills advertising the Battle of the Bands.

"Look, they're fabulous, and we're desperate. I know how you feel about them," Tommy whispered, "about their not becoming a freak show and everything. But they can be themselves in a rock band and no one will think they're strange at all."

"Want to bet?" I challenged him.

"Well, what I mean is, people expect weirdness from rock bands. It's perfect for them."

Tommy was actually right about that. People did expect weirdness from rock bands, so it might not turn out so bad to have them in the band.

The kids had finished singing. The backup band bowed and filed off the stage. Lupi placed an odd-shaped hat on the corner of the stage. I guessed that she'd seen the other bands do this to encourage the audience to put money into the hat.

But instead, Drake took some of the handbills from the other band members and laid them down next to the hat. Then he sprinkled some of the yellow dust over the paper, turning it into dollar bills! Everyone gasped.

"What kind of trick is that?" someone cried out as Drake picked up the money and placed it into the hat. Then he passed the hat full of money to the audience.

"He's giving money away?" another person cried. "I thought he was going to pass the hat to try and *get* money!"

The crowd gathered around the hat and took turns pulling out dollar bills. People began laughing and throwing Drake's money in the air.

"Magic tricks in a rock band?" Iris exclaimed. "That's pretty cool."

Finally, one man was left holding the almost empty hat. A scream suddenly tore through the air. I turned in the direction of the scream and noticed that hundreds of spiders were crawling out of the hat and up the man's arm. Other people who had reached into the hat also started shaking spiders out of their clothes and brushing them off their arms. The mall echoed with shrieks.

"*Ahhh*! They're all over me!" somebody cried. "Keep your hands away from that hat!"

"That's pretty awful," Iris groaned, shuddering.

I watched as several people screamed and ran

away. I suddenly spotted the little man with dark glasses who had got his umbrella stuck on Lupi's ping-pong net. As soon as the spiders started taking over, he and that goofy-looking guy in the same plaid suit moved up to the stage to talk to Drake.

I sneaked close enough behind them so that I could hear what they were saying, but far enough away so that they wouldn't know I was eavesdropping.

"Look, I want to know how you do that trick with the money," the man in the plaid suit said urgently.

"I told you, it's the same potion I used last time," Drake replied solemnly.

The funny-looking man's eyes darted this way and that, scanning the mall with suspicion. "Can you do it with these leaflets?" he whispered.

"Sure." I briefly saw a photo of the man in the same plaid suit on the leaflets, just before Drake sprinkled his yellow dust on them. But before I could read what was printed on them, they turned into dollar bills.

The man's eyes widened and he elbowed his friend. "Wow! What a great trick! If we could get our hands on some of that potion, we'd have it made! Okay, kid, where can we get some of this potion?" He rubbed his hands together gleefully.

Just as Drake opened his mouth to answer, the short man grabbed the handful of money from his friend and started to shove it into his own pocket.

"Oh, no, you don't," the man in the plaid suit

snarled through gritted teeth. He pulled the little man up roughly by the front of his shirt, almost lifting him off his feet. "They were my leaflets, so it's my money! Give it back . . . now! It's mine."

I was a little startled by all this. I didn't know what it was, but this man seemed desperate about something. Just then, Lupi tugged at my sleeve, drawing me away from where Drake and the two men stood.

"How did you like the show, Samantha?" she asked.

"It was really great, Lupi, really. You and Drake are getting really good. And the crowd loved you."

"You were fabulous," Tommy agreed. Lupi grinned with satisfaction.

"Such a charming performance, don't you think so, Samantha?" asked Dr Brown, who wore an antique dress that matched Lupi's.

"Uh, yes. Charming." I introduced Dr Brown and Mr Brown to Tommy and Iris.

As Drake joined us, I noticed the two strangers walking away from the stage. The man in the plaid suit was clutching on to a fistful of dollar bills and slapping away the outstretched hands of his little friend.

"The spiders would look terrific in a video," said Drake.

"Yes, I quite agree — they were so well behaved," Mr Brown added.

"My mother wouldn't think so," Iris muttered.

The Browns gave her a curious look. Then they all shook hands and we said good-bye.

"See you tomorrow," I called to the children.

Once we were outside, Tommy, who worked on the school paper, told me, "Nobody's covered the contest yet for the *Davis Leader*, so I'm going to write an article about it."

He shoved some coins into a newspaper machine and pulled out a copy of the Plainview paper. The headline proclaimed the county's forthcoming election, centred above the pictures of the candidates.

Tommy scanned the headline and shoved the paper under his arm. "So what about inviting the Browns to play in our band?" he asked.

"I think they're terrific. We have a pretty good chance of winning if they join our band," I told him, even though I still felt nervous about the idea.

"Look, I just want to be famous," Iris broke in. "I want to quit my job and be somebody. But tell the Browns not to bring any spiders or creepy stuff, okay?"

"Okay," I assured her, but only I knew how hard it would be to keep that kind of thing from happening.

Chapter 5

I PLANNED TO lure Iris to my house to surprise her on her birthday. Actually I had invited a bunch of friends, who had already gathered there when Iris called.

"I have to work, can you believe it?" she cried. "Boy, what I put up with just for money."

"I have an idea, Iris." I motioned for the roomful of people to be quiet. "What time do you get off work?"

"Ten o'clock," she told me.

"Okay, we'll, I mean, I'll see you then."

After we gathered up the cake, ice-cream, and gifts, my mother drove us all down to Burger Headquarters. At ten o'clock we walked through the door — ten people adorned with funny hats, streamers, and blowers, all singing happy birthday.

Iris, busy dealing with an irate customer when we walked into the restaurant, brightened when she saw us lugging in the cake lit with candles. "Hey, listen," she invited her customer, "why don't you sit down and have some cake with us while you wait for your order."

"I'll spoil my appetite," the woman replied petulantly.

"Oh, come on," Iris urged. "My uncle Horace always used to say that cake was good for the soul."

I laughed, hearing Iris quoting one of her crazy relatives again. Iris had a whole repertoire of relative stories. I suppose her customer thought Iris was pretty funny too, because she sat down with us at one of the tables.

Iris came out from behind the counter and hugged me. "I should've have known. What a pal."

"Blow out the candles, Iris," insisted Maurice Maklowitz, a boy who had a crush on me. "The wax is dripping all over the cake."

Allison Rumby, Shannon Blackwell, and Randy Alsip, who wore his hat on his face as though it were a nose, joined Maurice in urging Iris to blow out the candles.

"This is the best birthday." Iris grinned as I handed her the cake cutter. "Can I take your order please?"

We laughed. I offered to cut the cake for her since she already spent so much of her time serving food, but she wanted to do it herself. After everybody had eaten a piece of cake, Iris opened her presents. She loved the T-shirt I had chosen for her. The boys had bought her an album that she liked, Allison gave her a necklace, and Shannon gave her a poster of her favourite rock star. Tommy took a picture of all of us with the cardboard cutout of Ham Burger, the Burger Headquarters' mascot. Then Iris climbed up on top of one of the tables and made an announcement.

"I want to welcome you all to this celebration of my birthday and my new career as a rock singer. Sam, Tommy, and I have started a band with some other kids, and we're entering the Battle of the Bands. We're going to be a real hit, so come and hear us sing."

Everybody clapped and whooped. "Let's hear you sing now!" Maurice cried.

Iris wasn't at all shy, so she immediately launched into a popular song. She sounded really good, too. Her years in the choral group had really paid off.

The next day I bought the Browns over to Tommy's house after school so we could try to blend them into the band with Tommy, Iris and me.

After talking about what songs we might like to rehearse, Drake pulled out a conch shell from his satchel full of tricks and began to blow on one end of it, as though it were a horn. The sound that came out was haunting and primitive, and Lupi joined in with what she called a whistle flute from Mexico that was made of clay. Iris ran into the kitchen to get some spoons. Then Lupi started singing, her voice studded with little pops and gasps that matched the array of background sounds Drake and Iris were producing. After they ended the song with a long note on the conch shell, Tommy and I applauded wildly.

"It really sounds different," I said. "There won't be another band like us in the whole world."

Drake, who had got really involved in electronic devices, brought out a tape player and turned it on. A loud creak came from the tape machine.

"What's that?" we asked

"A coffin opening," Drake answered seriously. "And listen to this, I love this."

Sirens screeched through the room. As I clamped my hands over my ears, Lupi started to laugh.

"Don't you like them?" Drake asked me

"There great!" Tommy shouted.

The other sounds on the tape included crickets, a chain saw, and the piranhas eating their lunch.

"You don't really have piranhas, do you?" asked Iris when Drake explained the sound of thrashing in water that we heard.

"Yes, and they're adorable," Lupi told her. "Their names are Tobias, Carno, and Pesky."

"I didn't know you had named them." I smiled at my friends.

"They must be really fashionable pets." Iris suddenly started to chuckle. "I remember my aunt Mavis bought an ocelot once because it was fashionable, but it chewed up all of the furniture."

"I want to use these sounds in a video," Drake announced. "I want to earn enough money so that I can make one of our group."

"What a great idea," Tommy agreed. "Maybe we can put our money together, or use the prize money — if we win."

"Well, I have my babysitting money and my

allowance," I offered.

"And I have my job at Burger Headquarters," Iris said. "At least until we get really famous."

"We'll probably need extra money for costumes and music, too," Tommy pointed out.

"We can use costumes from our parents' collection," Lupi suggested. "We don't have any money at all, but we can see that it's something everyone wants to have."

"You sort of can't live without it," I informed her.

I sat down at the piano and played some notes so that Tommy could tune his guitar. He and I played a song while Iris sang. Then Lupi played a small lyre and Drake hummed along. The combination really sounded interesting.

"I love the way we sound," I told them when we had finished playing.

"We have to think of a name for our band," Iris insisted.

"Blood," said Drake, staring at his finger, which he had just cut on the edge of some sheet music.

"Blood?" We all looked at each other in confusion. I had been thinking of something more like The Sensational Samantha Slade Band or The One in a Million Band, but Blood?

"I think it's a great name," said Tommy.

"Me, too," Lupi agreed.

Iris wrinkled her nose, but when she saw how excited everyone else was about the name, she said okay.

"I think we're a winning combination," Tommy exclaimed, and we went around slapping each other's palms. Lupi and Drake endured the hand slapping, but looked at us curiously until we had finished.

"It's a commom custom," Tommy explained. "People do that when they're happy about the way something has worked out."

After the rehearsal Iris and I took the Browns to their house, where I would babysit them until their parents got home.

As Iris continued on to work, the kids and I walked up the front path. I was the first to notice a yellow envelope peeking out from underneath the door. I knelt to pick it up. It was addressed to "Drake".

I handed it to him. "For you."

He slit the envelope open and silently read the typewritten note. Then he read it aloud to Lupi and me: "Meet me next to the yellow dustbin across the street from your house on Saturday night. I'll be wearing something yellow."

"Who wrote it?" I asked.

"It doesn't say. Maybe it's the same person who offered to pay me for the money potion when we played in the mall."

"Somebody offered to *pay* you?" I asked incredulous.

"Yes," Drake answered matter-of-factly.

"What did this person look like?" Lupi and I asked at the same time.

"Well, you remember those two men I talked to, Samantha — the one in the plaid suit and the other one who got his umbrella caught in our ping-pong net," Drake explained. "The one in the plaid suit offered to pay me."

I gulped. "I saw him snatch the money you made away from the shorter one. Why, I'll bet he even planned that whole thing with his friend and the umbrella," I said dramatically. "How did he know where you live?"

Drake shrugged. "Maybe he asked somebody, or maybe he followed us home. I think he must be very tricky."

Lupi leaned over his shoulder to read the note. "Why would he want the money potion? What would he use it for?"

"I don't know. Maybe he's in debt or he needs the money for some life-saving operation. Whatever it is, he must be desperate. We have to find out who he is and what he really wants." As I spoke, a chill zoomed through me.

Chapter 6

WE REHEARSED EVERY day from Monday until Friday, the day of our first performance. Everthing seemed to be going smoothly, so by Friday we felt nervous but ready to go.

"Ten green bottles, hanging on the wall," Iris, Tommy, Patrick, and I sang on the way to the Palladium in Clearville, the site of our first performance. My mother was driving while my father catnapped.

"I thought you'd want to save your voices," Mum suggested.

"Now that's a good idea," Iris agreed, but we all started talking anyway. Somehow talking seemed to take away the jitters.

Patrick, my bratty little brother, told us jokes that he had learned from his new joke book — and they weren't the least bit funny.

"What goes like this?" Patrick put his fingertips together, palms nearly touching but curving as though he were holding a baseball.

We all gave up. "I don't know. What?"

"A spider doing pushups on a mirror."

Well, I told you they weren't very funny.

The Browns were travelling to the concert

with their own parents. I worried about their getting there and finding the place — or worse, getting there and turning the whole place upside down before we had a chance to perform.

As it turned out, the Browns had arrived before us, and as we drove up, we saw them walking around the Palladium, apparently as calm as could be. From the outside the Palladium looked like a large sparkling grey dome, surrounded by an expanse of cement.

My parents dropped us off in front of the stage entrance and went to park the car.

"Hi, Lupi. Hi, Drake," I greeted them.

"Hi, everybody." Lupi, dressed in a leather and fur outfit, grinned up at us. Drake, wearing a hat with bones hanging from the brim and an antique black suit, carried a big burlap sack over his shoulder.

"What's in the bag, Drake?" I asked. I could see that whatever he had in the bag was moving.

"It's a suprise. You'll see," he answered mysteriously.

I didn't have time to worry about it because we still had to rehearse before our performance. We walked into the Palladium. We stood for a moment in the entrance of the vast round auditorium, staring at the stage in amazement. I wondered whether the audience would fill up all that empty space.

Tommy, Iris, and I found the dressing rooms and changed into our stage clothes. I wore my mother's old orange sequined prom dress, Iris wore the T-shirt I had given her with some bright orange glittery tights, and Tommy wore an antique suit like the one Drake wore — compliments of the Browns' old clothing collection. When we looked at ourselves in a full-length mirror, we decided we all looked pretty original.

Then we went out onto the stage to join the others. Drake, already playing the flute, was standing next to the burlap bag, which was still moving around. There was definitely something alive in it.

"I never know what to expect from you guys," Tommy said warily, looking at the bag.

"That's one thing you can count on with the Browns," I told him, laughing.

I sat down at the piano and began to play a few notes. Tommy tuned his guitar to the piano and we began to play together. Then Iris, Lupi and Drake sang along. We practised the hard parts of all the songs we planned to perform.

We were pretty involved in our music and didn't hear Monica and Sylvie Addams breeze into the backstage area. Monica came out to the wings of the stage to see us, her guitar slung across her back, looking as if she were a real pro at this kind of thing. Sylvie followed her loyally.

"Oh, hi, guys." She smiled her toothpaste-commercial smile at us. "What's going on?"

"Hopefully, we are," I answered.

"I'm on first," she announced proudly. "We're called The Spectaculars."

"Congratulations," I said. "I haven't had a chance to see the programmes yet."

"What's your group called?" Sylvie asked.

"Blood," Iris told her.

Monica wrinkled her nose in distaste. "Yuk."

"Knock 'em dead, Monica," Tommy said.

"Yeah, you too," she replied. With a toss of her ponytail, she flounced off towards the dressing rooms.

We practised a little bit more until Mr Spenck, one of the organizers of the Battle of the Bands, asked us to go backstage and wait to be called.

"This is it, gang," said Tommy.

Tommy and Iris went out to collect some programmes for the rest of us. We were featured right after The Spectaculars. The other groups, including The Yellow Jackets, whom we'd seen in the mall, sounded interesting, too. I scanned the list of their names: Minus One, The Winston Binston Band, Sitting Down, Rainbow Tree.

We all waited in an area backstage where we could peek out and see the other performers. I could feel myself getting nervous as the announcer began to talk.

"Tonight we'll all be hearing the debuts of the following bands: The Spectaulars, Blood, The Yellow Jackets, Minus One, The Winston Binston Band, Sitting Down, and Rainbow Tree.

"First, we have The Spectculars, a group that promises to live up to its name." Enthusiastic applause followed. "And now, with great pleasure, I'd like to introduce . . . The Spectaculars!"

The crowd went crazy. From our place behind the curtains we could see the group file out from the other side of the stage, dressed as exotic birds, their costumes made of real feathers of iridescent blues and greens. Monica's outfit was the grandest of all — she had this huge blue-green plume headdress that bobbed over her eyebrows when she walked.

Tommy whistled.

"Look at our feathered friends," gasped Iris.

"They look like real South American birds," said Lupi.

I looked at her. "Now, how would you know that?" I asked.

"We know many birds from that area. Monica looks authentic," she replied.

I was often surprised at the kind of information these kids seemed to pick up.

Monica and the band got themselves set up and then began to play. She started off with a really wild song. Then they did one where she and the other band members took turns leaving their instruments and acting as though they were flying. Their costumes, complete with feathered wings, almost made the illusion look real. And their voices even seemed birdlike.

"I wish we'd thought of that," moaned Iris.

"But we thought of this instead," Lupi reminded her.

Sometimes, surprisingly, Lupi and Drake seemed more levelheaded than normal people, I thought.

The Spectaculars really were spectacular, and the crowd went wild. We all felt a little nervous about coming in on the heels of such a great success.

"And now, let me present a group with a memorable name: Blood," said the announcer. "I don't know why they called themselves

Blood, but word has it they have a great sound. Let's hear it for . . . Blood!"

Everyone in the audience was in high spirits, enthusiastically welcoming us onto the stage. Drake dragged his burlap bag, which seemed to have calmed down since we had arrived, behind him.

I went straight to the piano, trying not to look directly at the huge audience. Lupi and Iris positioned themselves in front of one of the microphones, and Tommy and Drake, playing the guitar and conch shell, stood at the other.

The haunting tone of the conch sounded hollow in the vast auditorium. The audience listened with rapt attention. The piano and guitar created a soft accompaniment, and Lupi's strange, soaring voice shimmered above all the other sounds. Then Iris came in with her clear, playful alto, finishing the song on a long high note.

Applause rose from the crowd. While they were still clapping, we launched into the next song. It was a snappy, popular song featuring the piano, flute, guitar, and three voices. Tommy sang part of it by himself, then Lupi and Iris joined in.

While we were singing our last song, with Iris on the spoons and Lupi playing the jaws harp, Drake scurried over to the burlap bag, which he had left at the side of the stage. The rest of us were so involved in our singing that we didn't notice anything unusual until the crowd began to point and gasp and scream.

Suddenly Iris dropped her spoons with a clatter and ran over to the piano.

"Sam, look at that . . . snake!" she hissed.

I turned and saw Drake coming towards us carrying the family boa constrictor.

"Oh, no, Lawrence!" I cried.

"Lawrence?" questioned Iris.

"That's the snake's name," I explained. Iris covered her face with her hands. It was time for my solo, so I turned my attention away from her. No matter what, I figured the show had to go on. The snake, about twelve feet long with brown stripes along its back, wrapped itself around Drake's shoulder and gazed out over the crowd, flicking its forked tongue.

People began screaming, jumping up from their chairs, backing towards the exits. Iris sank down next to me on the piano bench.

"Sam, tell him to get that snake out of here!" she cried. "I can't stand snakes! I'm allergic to them."

"*You* tell him," I objected. "*I'm* playing the piano." I didn't want to get caught in the middle of this.

Monica peered from the wings, shrieking her head off. If she had got any louder, no one would have been able to hear our playing. But we kept on playing just the same. Lawrence the boa arched its body majestically, making the most of the moment.

Drake petted Lawrence affectionately, but the reptile, apparently very curious about its surroundings, slithered to the floor and headed for the audience, creating even more chaos. Lawrence didn't seem to mind that the entire audience had either left their chairs screaming or sat in stunned silence because of its appearance. Lawrence was a very social snake.

"Drake, catch the snake!" I cried form the piano bench.

Just as Lawrence started to slither happily down the staircase from the stage, Drake grabbed its tail and pulled. I could see that Lawrence, who was very strong, was resisting, but I turned back to the piano because I felt we had to end the performance on the right note. Lupi and Tommy were still singing beautifully, but Iris, who had picked up her spoons again, couldn't seem to find the right rhythm. She kept her eyes fixed on Lawrence the whole time.

As we built our song to a climax, I looked over and I saw Drake lift the boa onto his shoulder. Lawrence flicked his tongue at his audience, some of whom laughed while others simply shuddered. When we came to the end of our song, applause filled the auditorium.

I stood between Lupi and Drake as we all took our bows, even the boa.

"Lawrence thinks the ovation is for him," Lupi whispered to me.

When we got backstage, my parents and Patrick were waiting to congratulate us.

"Let me pet the boa," cried Patrick. He started asking Drake a lot of questions about Lawrence.

"Samantha, it was a wonderful performance, but why in the world did you bring a *snake* onstage?" my mother wanted to know.

"It wasn't my idea," I admitted.

"I used to collect snakes when I was a boy," my father reminisced, stroking Lawrence. "This one is a terrific specimen."

"Wow, really?" I exclaimed. It amazed me what I learned about my parents sometimes. It was as if they had this whole history without me. "Why didn't you ever tell me that?"

Dad shrugged. "It never came up in conversation."

Tommy ran over to us and held out his hand. "Give me five."

I slapped his palm, and so did Iris. Lupi and Drake watched this exchange with great interest.

We stuck around to see the other bands perform. I liked Minus One and Rainbow Tree the best. Rainbow Tree, a group of kids dressed in rainbow leotards with rainbow-painted instruments, received a huge ovation, bigger than either The Spectaculars or Blood.

Finally we packed up our instruments and made our way outside. Because I had left some schoolwork at their house, I decide to ride home with the Browns. But I hadn't planned on drawing a crowd with my exit.

A large group of people had gathered around the Browns' odd looking car: a long, black hearse. Of course, since it was their car, it wasn't even ordinary for a hearse. The body looked as if it belonged on a horse-drawn hearse carriage, but had been mounted on top of a motor-driven cab. And they had decorated the hearse's curtains with hanging bones and sharp little teeth.

When we arrived, Dr Brown put the car in the garage and I went inside to find my schoolwork. When I came back outside, I saw Drake standing across the street near the yellow dustbin, talking to a man who wore dark glasses. The man looked familiar — he was the little guy who had got tangled up in the ping-pong net. He must have been the one who had sent Drake the note! I stood nearby, waiting for Drake to finish talking. Suddenly the man looked up and saw me watching them. He whispered one last thing to Drake, then quickly turned and left.

"Drake!" I called, running over to him. "Who was that?"

"The man who sent me the note," he explained. "He wants me to help his candidate win an election. I told him I would."

"He wants an eight-year-old boy to help him win an election? Because you can make money?"

"Yes. And he'll pay me, Sam. We can use money to make a video. We need a camera, remember?"

"But you can make money just by sprinkling your potion on things," I reminded him. "What do you need his money for?"

"I don't know if we should really spend my money. The potion dissolves after a while."

"Wow. Does this guy know that?" I asked.

"He didn't ask, so I guess he didn't think it was important. He just said he wanted the money potion."

I shook my head in disbelief. I knew Drake hadn't kept this information from the man due to dishonesty; he just accepted what the man had said word for word. It didn't even occur to him that he was being paid money for the potion because the two men thought it would make them even more money — *real* money, not money that would dissolve. "What election is this for? Did he tell you?"

"I think he said county supervisor," Drake answered thoughtfully. "What do supervisors do?"

"I'm not really sure," I replied, feeling really puzzled. "Look, this guy sounds like a complete wacko. From what I've seen of the two guys at the mall, they have violent tempers, and that scares me. We've got to find out who this candidate is."

A county election candidate who wanted a small boy to help him win? It sounded really impossible.

Chapter 7

THE NEXT MORNING I picked up the newspaper after my mother had finished with it. Mainly I wanted to check out the candidates to see who was running for office.

Four candidates were running for county supervisor: Donna Arillo, Courtney Braxton, Lee Becker, and a dark horse candidate named Mark Hester. All except Hester had their photographs in the paper.

I had heard of Mark Hester: he wanted to turn Jones Park, which my Social Action Committee had worked so hard on, into a convention centre. I didn't like him for that, but I knew that alone didn't make him a bad person. Besides, I had never even seen him.

I decided to ask my parents. "What do you know about the candidates for supervisor?" I asked my mum.

"Well, the worst one is Hester, if you ask me, but fortunately he doesn't have a chance of winning. Arillo and Becker are my favourites of the bunch. Arillo is a pharmacist and Becker is a lawyer. Braxton is a professor at the university."

"But what are their characters like?" I
pressed.

"Well, Hester's been on the city council of
Plainview," she began, "so I know a little more
about him. The other candidates are all from
out of town, so I don't know as much about
their characters. I do know that Becker has a
good reputation as a lawyer, and Braxton's
classes are alway full at the university. Hester
resigned from the city council when he was
accused of using city funds for his own needs.
He got voted onto the council only because he
ran unopposed. But I doubt he'll get anywhere
in this election. He's one of these people who try
lots of different schemes and never succeed. I
heard that he started out as a car salesman, but
the cars he sold needed hundreds of dollars'
worth of repair work. Then he thought he could
get rich quick by investing in real estate, except
he ran out of money and they say he started
selling parcels of land that didn't exist, although
no one ever caught him at it. He opened shops
and petrol stations that lost money and went
bankrupt, and he borrowed lots of money and
almost never paid it back. I think now he seems
really desperate to fix up his image and finally
be somebody. He fell into politics by accident
and now he's going to try to make the most of it.
Whether they're all true or not, I'm inclined to
believe the rumours about him. I get the feeling
that he's a real snake."

Patrick giggled. "Oh, like Lawrence."

Mum and I looked at each other and laughed.

"He's a little different from Lawrence,"
Mum told him. "I think I like Lawrence better.

And Lawrence seems more intelligent."

"So you think he's capable of bad things?" I asked.

Mum shrugged. "It's hard to say. He's such a jerk that most of his schemes fall through. But he causes a lot of trouble all the same. I'm willing to trust my instincts — which tell me *not* to trust him. And I don't think it would do the county any good to have him in office."

That was enough for me. Hester certainly sounded like the kind of candidate who might be crazy enough to ask Drake for potions. My mum had good instincts where people's characters were concerned. I guess that's why she never said anything about the Browns' weirdness. She knew that deep down inside they were good people, no matter how odd they seemed.

I babysat for the Browns that night. I brought my music along just in case we had an opportunity to rehearse. When I arrived, a sign affixed to the front door read: "Sam, we are having a music lesson with Antonia. Come around to Uncle Tompkins' room."

I shuddered at the mention of Antonia. As usual, I edged around the trapdoor as I entered the house. I followed the staircase upward to Uncle Tompkins' room, but somewhere I guess I took a wrong turn. In the dark hall all the rooms looked alike from the outside. Finally I thought I heard Antonia's voice, and I headed in that direction.

I opened a door and stepped inside. Or rather, I stepped down. I gasped. Hissing rose around me like the hiss of steam. I screamed.

The floor slithered beneath my shoes as though it were alive. I reached out towards the wall to get my balance, but I had already moved too far from the wall. I teetered on the balls of my feet, trying not to fall over. Something slippery tried to wriggle up my trouser leg. I looked down, my eyes gradually adjusting to the darkness. The sunken floor was covered with a writhing mass of snakes. I couldn't stop screaming then, but I couldn't get out either. Each time I tried to take a step, a snake would slither into the space where I had intended to put my foot. I just stood there, my feet planted in the midst of them, letting them glide over my shoes. Each time one tried to move up my leg, I would just about die.

What if they were poisonous? What if they bit me and I just died here, lying in the middle of all of them? I wondered frantically. The Browns *could* have poisonous snakes — they probably found them very exciting.

While I stood there, praying that somebody would hear my screams, I suddenly smelled and heard something. A figure filled the open doorway. All the air seemed to leave the room as Uncle Tompkins trudged steadily towards me.

He stepped right on the snakes, obviously unmindful of them, his arms outstretched to me. I wanted to avoid him — I couldn't stand being touched by him — but it was no use. I couldn't move. I held my breath, gagging from the smell. He was right next to me and then worse — he picked me up in his cold, dead arms. He lifted me several inches above the hissing snakes and carried me out of the room.

Then he slammed the door to the snake pit, deposited me on the floor of the hallway, and stood looking down at me.

"*Uhhhhh*," was all he said, staring at me with his one unblinking eye, his wrappings fluttering around him.

I remembered that he didn't like my screaming very much. It made him very nervous.

"Samantha, are you okay?" Lupi cried as she ran towards me.

I propped myself on my elbows, swallowing the urge to throw up. "Yes, I'm fine now. Uncle Tompkins rescued me from the snakes."

"Isn't he a sweetheart?" she exclaimed, tugging affectionately at his torn wrapping. "It's a good thing Drake asked him to come up here to put some of Uncle's moans and groans on a sound effects tape."

Uncle Tompkins groaned. I wouldn't exactly call him a sweetheart, but it was nice of him to drag me out of the snake pit.

"Why do you have all those snakes in that room?" I asked Lupi.

"Oh, that's for the tape too. We decided to have our own snake pit so that we could record some really good sound effects for the group," explained Lupi. "Especially since some people didn't like Lawrence, the recording seemed like a good idea. And with you screaming in the middle of it, it should be super!"

"I'm glad I was such a hit," I muttered, dragging myself to my feet. "Are they poisonous?"

"No, they're not." Lupi almost looked

disappointed. "They're only garter snakes. The most they might do is bite if you stepped on them."

I nearly fainted at the thought. I might have stepped on five or six of them at once. What if they had all bitten me?

Uncle Tompkins shuffled down the hall away from us, his smell trailing behind him.

Drake and Antonia were waiting for us in the music room. Antonia's eyes glittered when she saw me. "So, you have come for your music lesson."

"Well, actually, no," I stammered. "I came to babysit."

"I do not need a babysitter," Antonia replied. "But I'm parched. Perhaps you have something for someone very thirsty."

"Not me," I quickly replied. "Look in the kitchen."

She ambled off down the hall, chattering to herself.

Drake greeted me excitedly. "As soon as we have enough money for a video camera, we'll make a video of the snake pit. Maybe you'd like to star in it, Samantha."

"No, thanks, Drake," I told him. "Once is enough."

"Just listen to yourself, Sam," he insisted. "You did this so well. I think these are your best screams."

He replayed the tape for all of us to hear. We heard the hissing of the snakes, the sound of my screaming, then Uncle Tompkins' heavy footsteps and his groans as he lifted me out of there. I could even hear the sound of my gagging at his stench.

I clamped my hands over my ears so that I wouldn't have to listen. Hearing made me remember it all too clearly. I just wanted to forget about it.

That night when I went home, my father asked me what that horrible smell was.

"Oh, I don't know, Dad," I answered. "Must be something in the air."

"Wow, it's awful. Like skunk. Maybe someone ran over a skunk outside," he guessed.

I showered, scrubbing myself vigorously to get the smell of Uncle Tompkins off me. All my clothes smelled like him, too, so I shoved them in the washing machine. Finally I tried to fall asleep. But I kept dreaming that I was in the snake pit and that I had fallen down. Thousands of snakes crawled over me, and I knew that if I moved a muscle, one would bite me. I could even feel the sting of their bites all over me.

And then Uncle Tompkins rescued me. I woke up in a cold sweat, smelling him again.

I really couldn't decide which was worse: the wriggling mass of snakes under my feet or the sight and smell of that awful mummy.

Chapter 8

A WEEK OF rehearsals passed before our next performance. Because the second concert would be held near where Bubbles the monster lived, we arranged it so that the Browns drove all of us except Iris to the concert. We asked Dr and Mr Brown if we could stop off at Mt. Monk to see Bubbles and her new baby.

"I have to give Bubbles and the baby some more invisibilty formula," Drake explained.

Early that afternoon, we all climbed out of the hearse at the base of the mountain where we had last seen the monster. Patches of melting snow lay upon the ground. The oak and birch trees looked bare and stark against the grey sky. We had been here just a few months earlier, but the snow-covered summit looked very different this time.

We hiked up the mountain. We had to guess where Bubbles might be, hoping that she had stayed close to where we had left her with her baby.

Tommy discovered a trail of fresh monster prints that we followed up the mountain. The trail was easy going for the first half hour, but then it turned into a long, hard hike up the side of the mountain. We scaled the steep surfaces of rock and boulders, our mittened hands grabbing for purchase on the slippery rocks. At one point Drake slid on his belly several yards down the incline. At times the trail seemed almost unrecognizable, but finally near the top it levelled out and travel became easier.

Near the top of the mountain we spotted Bubbles, munching on some evergreen trees, her baby by her side. Bubbles was greenish brown, about twenty-five feet long and fifteen feet from head to toe. She had a long thin neck, long tail, and a thundering, thick body that hung close to the ground. She looked a little like a common dinosaur, the brontosaurus, except not as big. Her baby, although a shade paler than Bubbles, was an exact replica of her mother. She even copied Bubbles' way of eating, except that she had to wait for her mother to pick the juiciest branches from the treetops and hand them down to her.

"What should we name the baby, Samantha?" Lupi asked me, because I had given Bubbles her name.

Suddenly the baby let out a loud burp and we all giggled.

"Maybe we should call her Burp," I suggested.

"It has a nice ring to it," Tommy agreed, laughing.

When Bubbles noticed us, she approached and wrapped her long neck around each of us in turn. She licked my face with her big tongue and honked loudly.

"The baby is such a beautiful specimen," cried Mr Brown excitedly.

Drake sprinkled the blue invisibility formula on the animals and then joined Lupi in singing a song for the monsters. When they had finished their song, we kissed both Bubbles and Burp good-bye and trekked back down the mountainside.

When we arrived at the concert hall, Iris was waiting for us.

"I started to wonder whether you would show up at all," she said. "I thought I would have to be a single red blood cell."

"Well, you can relax now," Tommy reassured her. "The rest of the bloodstream is here."

We went back to the dressing rooms (just one for the boys and one for the girls) and got dressed in our outfits — the boys in their antique suits with red cutout hearts pinned to their chests. Lupi, Iris, and I had decided to wear red outfits so that we all matched and made people think of "Blood". We even wore drops of red food colouring on our cheeks, which I thought looked really wild.

Drake carried a large box in from the car.

"That's not another snake, is it?" Iris asked warily. "I'm telling you, Drake, if I see one more creepy thing around here, I'm out of this band."

"Don't worry, Iris," he answered sweetly. "This creature is one you won't even have to see."

I frowned at him.

"Samantha, you've already met this one," he

said. "We have to transport him in a music box."

I guessed that it was Muki, the creature that lived in the clavichord.

"If it's a mouse, get it out of here," Iris insisted hotly.

"It's more like a Mexican hairless dog," I told her. "But the piano will sound wonderful."

Iris looked at me as though I'd lost a substantial part of my brain. "Well, my cousin Lucia had a Mexican hairless once. It barked and shivered all the time, as though it were cold. She had to keep it wrapped up in blankets."

This time, we were on before Monica, and Drake placed Muki in the piano when no one except Lupi and I was looking. We started our performance with me soloing on the piano and Lupi and Drake doing a strange dance across the stage. The tone of the piano became a bright shimmer with Muki inside, and the sound seemed to have a hypnotic effect on the two Brown children. They danced trancelike, as though they were doing a minuet, but with fixed, doll-like expressions on their faces.

"We didn't rehearse this," Iris whispered next to me.

"*Shhh*, it looks good," I whispered back.

Then Lupi and Drake began to clap together some sticks that looked like bones. We had never rehearsed a rhythm like that, and I couldn't follow it, so I just had to let them carry on.

The crowd loved the song — if you could call it that. Next Iris sang a popular song, and we all played with her. Drake performed on the flute, dancing in the same hypnotic manner, with Lupi following him while she sang.

When we finished playing, Drake lifted the piano lid and took Muki out. The little creature blinked sorrowfully at the audience.

"Tuck him under your arm," I suggested. "People might see him and want to know what it is."

"If they really want to know, I can tell them," Drake said solemnly, but he did as he was told.

We left the stage with applause ringing in our ears. Once backstage, Drake lowered Muki back into the music box.

"Wow, they loved it, Samantha!" cried Tommy. "We're a hit."

"Just think, soon I'll be able to quit my job at Burger Headquarters." Iris sighed dreamily.

"Let's not rush things," I warned.

Monica and her group strode towards us in a cloud of feathers. "Nice work, Blood," she said sarcastically, "but it didn't sound like real music to me."

"We were experimenting," Lupi explained.

"The judges probably thought you were doing a comedy act," Monica snorted as she and the others breezed past us.

The Spectaculars played even more spectacularly than they had the first time. They even plucked a few feathers from their plumage and threw them at the audience, who reached out to catch them.

After the rest of the show, I found Lupi and Drake signing autographs outside the dressing rooms.

"There's no writing on mine!" a fan complained.

complained.

"I used disappearing ink," Lupi declared proundly. "It comes and goes."

I changed back into my normal clothes and walked past the boys' dressing room. The door was open, but no one answered my knock. I peered in and noticed a typewritten note propped up on the dresser closest to the door. The note read: "Drake: Please meet me in the South car park to give me the potion."

I swallowed hard. This was making me nervous. What was the formula this time? Had Drake made arrangements that I didn't know about? I went backstage to find him, but I guessed that he must have left for the car park already.

I ran over to the South car park, desperately looking for him.

Then I saw Drake walking towards a stranger who was dressed in a scarf and overcoat.

"Drake!" I called, running after him. He looked so small in the vast parking area, smaller that I had ever thought of him. He was so smart, I sometimes forgot he was still just a little boy. He started to turn around, but then the man motioned to him.

As I drew closer, I could see that the stranger had covered himself up so that he was unrecognizable. Out of breath, I came up alongside Drake.

"What potion does he want?" I asked.

Drake stopped and opened an envelope. He slid out a piece of paper with what looked like a glob of peanut butter attached to it. "He needs more of the money-making potion, but I ran out. I'll have to make some more. So I'm giving him this potion," he explained. "I think he can use it."

"You don't even know this person and you're giving away your secrets?" I screeched.

"I'm not *giving* them away," Drake reminded me. "I'm selling them. Don't worry, Samantha. It's just a job. At last I can earn some money for our video camera."

"But Drake, this is all wrong," I cried, running after him again. We had moved within earshot of the stranger, but I kept talking.

"What's your name?" I asked the man point-blank. I noticed it was the short man who had got his umbrella stuck in the ping-pong net.

"I don't need to tell you my name," he snarled into the muffler, which made his voice sound very strange.

"Don't worry, Samantha," Drake urged, handing the man the envelope and explaining that he didn't have any more of the money potion.

The man moved his muffler the tiniest bit so that he could sniff the envelope. He gave Drake a suspicious look.

"It smells like peanut butter," he said warily.

"The potion is mixed with peanut butter," Drake explained. "Have your candidate rub some on his cheeks and let it dry."

"Drake, you shouldn't have anything to do with this person again," I told him. Then I turned to the stranger. "Leave this boy alone, do you hear me? I don't want you to bother him again."

"Samantha, he has to pay me," Drake

insisted. The man hesitated for a moment, but then handed Drake an envelope. I suppose the guy figured that the money potion had worked so well, he ought to be able to trust this one too.

"No. Take the potion back and tell him to keep his money!" I cried, tugging at the envelope, which fell to the ground. The man stooped down and picked it up. While I was arguing, he deftly slipped the envelope into Drake's suit pocket and ran soundlessly to a nearby car. When I finally looked up, he was already driving off.

"Now look! He's got away!" I cried. " What are we going to do?"

"Samantha, don't worry," Drake tried to reassure me. "He just wants to help his candidate win an election."

"Yes, but anyone who would do a thing like this has to be the wrong kind of candidate, as far as I'm concerned," I replied. "I'm almost sure I know who the candidate is, and I don't think it's a good idea to help someone like him. You just don't know anything about the normal world!"

"But I'm learning," he insisted.

On the way home in the car, Drake described the potion he'd given the stranger. "It's peanut butter mixed with my mystery ingredient. It helped my rat, Trash, find his way through a complicated maze very quickly. I think it can work for people, too."

Tommy listened to our conversation with interest. The adults, involved in some other conversation, didn't hear us. "Who is this guy?" he asked.

Drake and I told him everything we knew

about the stranger and the candidate.

"Wow. Are you serious? This is a scandal. The candidate must be downright nuts to try something like this and think he can get away with it. If this guy has the money potion, he can buy everybody off. I guess that's one way to find your way through the political maze all right." Tommy laughed at his own joke.

I couldn't quite see the connection between Trash and the candidate, but then there are a lot of mysterious things about the way the Browns think. I know Drake doesn't understand winning and losing in the ordinary sense, but he *does* understand problem solving. The methods of problem solving used by the Browns, however, are quite different from anything you or I would come up with. For instance, when Drake gave me a Greatness Potion when I was running for president of my class, he didn't consider it a failure even after it turned me into a frog. He thought becoming a frog was great. And in a way, I suppose he was right. I learned that being small didn't mean being unimportant. I was smaller, with a different outside and a different appetite, but everything else about me was the same.

As we drove towards Plainview, I wondered what the peanut butter potion might do to the candidate. Maybe it would turn him into a rat.

Chapter 9

DURING SCHOOL ON Monday I was supposed to be thinking about an upcoming history test, but I couldn't stop thinking about the stranger. At lunch Iris and I got together in the library to study.

Monica glided over to us, grinning. "Hi, Iris, hi, Samantha," she whispered, because we were supposed to be quiet in the library. "You know, people have told me thay don't like Blood. They claim you're too sensationalistic."

"That's not true," we chorused.

"Well, I'm just telling you what some people say," she huffed defensively, before leaving us to join Sylvie Addams.

Iris and I looked at each other.

"Something's got to be done about her," Iris insisted.

"How can you do anything?" I asked. I used to like Monica before she became my rival. But I had become tired of her stuck-up attitude: she acted as if she thought she was better than everyone else.

"Do you think people are really saying that about us?" Iris asked me.

"No, she just made it up," I concluded. "*She* doesn't like us."

We left the library and walked down the hall. We saw Tommy walking towards us, but he looked as if he was in a hurry to get somewhere. We smiled at each other.

"Hi, Samantha, hi, Iris. How you doing?"

I noticed that he'd had his hair cut, so that I could finally see what his earlobes looked like. They looked wonderful. "Fine, how are you?" I asked.

"Good. See you at rehearsal." That was the end of our conversation.

Iris nudged me. "Couldn't you think of anything else to say?"

"What else could I say? I can't go running off at the mouth. It would look weird."

"You can too go running off at the mouth. I've seen you do it," she insisted. "And you could've said something really funny."

"Like what? Gee, I like your earlobes?" I spoke in a funny high voice.

We looked at each other and burst out laughing. We walked into class still laughing, and Ms Camacho, our maths teacher, scowled at us. Ms Camacho never seemed too approving of laughter, no matter what the reason, but she was especially disapproving when she didn't know what we were laughing about, or when we were laughing at her.

"Girls, settle down and take your seats," she said haughtily.

I clapped my hand over my mouth to keep from giggling and saw Iris' shoulders shaking ahead of me. I dared not look at her. If we looked at each other in this condition, there would be no holding us back.

Finally the moment passed. Ms Camacho started talking about binary numbers, which was enough to stifle any giggle. Binary numbers can be pretty interesting really, but my heart wasn't in it. And besides, I only considered myself a mathematician when it came to my own money.

The subject droned on and on. I stared out of the window, thinking about Blood.

"Samantha, what is the decimal equivalent of this number?" asked Ms Camacho, pointing to the 1001 she had written on the blackboard.

I started at the sound of my name. "Huh?"

Everyone cranked their heads around to stare at me. Wow, how embarrassing! I couldn't believe it. My face burned.

"I don't know," I mumbled.

"All right, Samantha. We realize that what's going on outside is far more interesting than the classroom, but we have work to do," Ms Camacho reminded me stuffily. "Monica, what is the answer?"

Monica beamed at me, then at Ms Camacho. I wanted to murder her. "Nine," she replied.

Ms Camacho smiled benevolently at Monica. Iris made a long pinched face, then stuck her finger in her mouth and pretended to gag.

"We've got to do something absolutely fabulous with Blood," I told Iris after class. "I can't stand the way Monica acts now that she's president *and* the lead singer of The Spectaculars."

"Think of something fast then," said Iris.

"So far, we've had a snake and some kind of creature in the piano. What next?"

"Oh, I'm sure we'll think of something."

Of course, I had no idea what that something would be.

At my house after school, Iris and I spread our homework out on the living room floor, along with a bag of potato crisps and a bottle of soda. When we had finished asking each other questions for our history test, we turned the TV on.

"Today in Plainview, county supervisor candidate Mark Hester introduced a new twist in his campaign during a speech to the Elks Club. It seems that Mr Hester has become something of a poet. Here's a segment from that speech given just two hours ago."

I couldn't believe what I saw — the same guy we had seen in the mall wearing that awful plaid suit beamed down at his audience from the podium. Wearing a dark suit this time, with his hair slicked down, he stood making a speech on TV! My hunch had been right: Mark Hester was the candidate buying potions from Drake! But I never would have guessed that Hester was the same guy we'd run into at the mall!

"Gosh, I never imagined that guy on TV!" I exclaimed. "It can't be the same person!" The memory of Hester roughing up the little man at the mall popped in my mind.

"*Shhh*," Iris hissed

Mark Hester could've passed for one of those guys who sell cars in the advertisements on the late show, but he sure didn't look like a county candidate. There was something sleazy about

Hester that defied decent clothes and a wet comb.

"Ladies and gentleman, as you can see, it is me, Mark Hester, and no court jester, here to make your lives better." Hester stopped momentarily, looking puzzled, as though he was a little scared that rhyming words had blurted out of his mouth. But the crowd laughed and applauded and Hester brightened suddenly, laughing himself, as if he had planned the whole speech this way. "I know it can be done, though I haven't yet won; it's only a matter of time, until you make your votes mine."

"Look at his expression!" noted Iris. "He seems suprised to hear the words coming out of his own mouth. I wonder who writes his speeches."

"I don't think anyone writes them," I told her. "I think it just happened to him."

"Don't tell me it's like magic, Samantha," Iris snorted. "Politicians don't eat cereal without checking with their campaign managers first. Remember how I was with you?"

"That was only for the seventh-grade class presidency," I reminded her. "And besides . . . " I stopped talking and listened to the rest of Hester's speech.

The crowd was on their feet, clapping enthusiastically. Hester grinned, forging ahead with great excitement.

"That's not what's on the slate, so I'm afraid I'll have to wait. I'd like to talk about crucial issues, but now I must look for a box of tissues . . . "

Iris burst out laughing. "I can't believe it. He's a real comedian."

Hester bowed to his audience, grinning like a maniac. You'd think he'd just won the Nobel Prize.

"Needless to say, that was the most successful speech Hester has given to date. Experts agree that this new rhyming style lends a more human and humorous quality to the candidate's otherwise drab presentations," noted the commentator. "Until today, Hester has been an extremely unpopular candidate. But what will happen now? Will Hester's new approach sway public opinion?"

"Now, how did he know that?" I muttered to myself.

"Know what?" Iris wanted to know.

"How did Drake, uh, Hester know that his speeches were drab?" I decided the mysterious little man must've told Drake about the candidate and asked him to keep Hester's presentation in mind. Or maybe it was just coincidental. After all, Drake had tried the potion on Trash, and the rat hadn't recited any poetry.

"I'm sure someone told him, Sam," Iris replied. "People generally complain loudly about politicians."

"Yeah, I guess you're right." Well, I had a lot of complaints about this one, but nothing that I could share with Iris. Obviously, Drake's potion had a much different effect on people than it did on rats.

After Iris went home, I called Drake to tell

him about the TV broadcast.

"That's so funny, Samantha." Drake giggled. "Trash didn't recite poetry at all. Maybe I'll give him some more of the potion and see if he does."

"But don't you understand, Drake? This means we know exactly who the candidate is. We met him in the mall, the funny-looking guy in the plaid suit. He's Mark Hester."

I went to babysit at the Browns' the next night. I took them shopping for a few items, but as soon as we left the grocery store, Drake said he wanted to go window-shopping for video cameras. When we got to the electronics place, though, he went inside and asked for a full demonstration.

He lifted the most expensive video camera and pretended to shoot Lupi and me. "Cut—take one. A little over to the left, Lupi."

"I see you've been reading up on this video stuff," I remarked.

"This is the exact same kind that The Screaming Meanies used to do their video," explained Drake. The Screaming Meanies are one of the kids' favourite rock groups.

I noticed the price tag spiraling from the camera handle. Eight hundred dollars! "I'd have to save my babysitting money for over a year to afford one of these," I exclaimed.

"But you won't have to." Drake smiled proudly. "I can earn enough money by selling four potions, as long as you don't keep making me give the money back."

I looked at him hard. "Do you mean to tell

me they're paying you two hundred dollars a potion?"

He nodded, grinning broadly. No wonder he had been so easily tempted, I thought.

Lupi sat down quietly, transfixed by ten different shows at the same time on a wall filled with nothing but televisions.

Finally I managed to get them out of there. But Drake couldn't think of anything else except the video camera all the way home. He even recited TV advertisements. "Try one for fifteen days—no home should be without one. It's the new idea in home movies. Become a videomaker in ten easy lessons."

While we were sitting down to dinner, the telephone rang. Drake stepped into the old black telephone booth in a dark corner of the kitchen.

"I'm glad you liked it," we heard Drake saying. "I've got a new batch of the money potion ready for you. I made quite a lot of it . . . well, soon . . . "

I realized that whoever was on the other end of the line sounded impatient. Lupi and I huddled into the phone booth next to Drake, so that the three of us could listen in on the conversation.

"I loved it!" the disguised voice exclaimed. "At first it was frightening talking in rhyme, but then I could sense that I had gained a power over the audience. It was so much fun! They loved me!"

Hester himself! "Where did you say you came from anyway, kid?" he rambled on. "And how do you come up with these magic potions?"

"I never told you where I'm from and I don't think you'd know the place anyway," Drake replied. "I make most of my potions in my own laboratory at home. It's an ability that runs in the family."

I thought Drake had revealed too much, so I interrupted. "If this is who I think it is, don't call here again. I don't want you asking Drake for any more formulas, do you understand?" I warned.

"Don't interfere, young lady," the muffled voice shot back. "Just stay out of this. People are finally paying attention to me. I'm having the best time of my life! These magic potions changed everything for me! People have finally started to see that I'm very necessary to this county — and to the world. I'm part of a grand design — you'll see. I'll fix up the county. I'm going to be powerful. This time, it'll really work. I'll have the money, prestige and charisma. Everyone will see that I'm a great man, a man of destiny," he went on, cackling gleefully, forgetting to disguise his voice. Then he stopped himself and warned, "You'd better not get in my way. This is none of your business."

"It *is* my business. *I'm* the babysitter. I'm responsible for these kids," I said huffily.

Hester hung up and a chill ran through me.

"Samantha's the babysitter! Samantha's the babysitter!" Lupi teased.

We all laughed, easing the tension a little, but I couldn't help thinking of Mark Hester. He must be really crazy. My hands were shaking. I felt relieved when Dr and Mr Brown came home.

I rushed up to them to tell them about the caller, but they didn't seem very disturbed by the news. Almost nothing bothered them.

Dr Brown smiled sweetly at her son. "Oh, I'm so pleased. This does sound exciting. Just think, our Drake with a real job!"

"That is fabulous, really," Mr Brown agreed. "It shows that he's fitting in here at last."

"But that's not it at all, Dr and Mr Brown." I tried to explain.

"Why does this disturb you so much, Samantha?" Mr Brown asked. He tipped his head first to one side and then the other, as if to get a better look at me.

"I'm worried because now that this politcal candidate had got hold of Drake's potions, he might use them for evil purposes," I blurted out.

The Browns looked at me with great interest.

"Evil purposes? I daresay that is exciting!" Dr Brown gasped. "Let's see how it all turns out, shall we?"

"Yes, lets see," Mr Brown added. "I'm very pleased with Drake's efforts."

Drake beamed at me. I could tell I wasn't going to win this round. I guessed they would have to "see" for themselves.

For the next few days we rehearsed in the afternoons. On Friday night I met the Browns at their house because we had planned to go to the concert together. Tommy's parents were driving him and Iris because they wanted to see the show, too. As I was locking my bike to their front gate. I could see Lupi and Drake trying to push Cousin Antonia back into the house.

I approached them reluctantly.

"Hi, Samantha," Lupi greeted me. "Cousin Antonia wants to go with us."

Antonia whirled around, flapping her raggedy arms. "Careful, I might bite you," she warned Lupi and Drake.

Lupi kept pushing her. She didn't seem at all afraid of Antonia. Finally she and Drake succeeded in coaxing the vampire into the house. We slammed the door behind her and ran to the car.

Dr Brown backed the car out of the driveway and drove slowly down the road. After about five miles, she noticed something fluttering in her rearview mirror.

"I daresay Cousin has followed us — she's climbed on the top of the car," Dr Brown remarked.

"Oh, no. Can't we take her home?" I cried.

"Samantha, if we turn around now, we'll be late," Mr Brown replied, consulting his watch. "I think it's more important that we get there on time."

After Dr Brown pulled the car to the side of the road, we all climbed out and dragged Antonia into the car. It seemed that wherever we wanted to put her, she resisted. She made herself as heavy as someone who was asleep — or dead! When we finally got her settled — in the back of the hearse, where the coffin would sit — I made sure I sat as far away from her as possible.

Antonia started to sing in her warbly, shrieky voice and kept it up until Lupi asked her if she would please stop. "Do save your voice, Antonia," Lupi suggested diplomatically.

"Does that mean I can sing with you?" Antonia asked. "I'm sure I'd be a wonderful addition."

I shuddered. She smelled like a thousand armpits.

"No, Antonia," said Drake. "We need you in the audience. You can listen to us and tell us how we sound."

When we arrived at the concert hall, Antonia, seeing people lined up outside, burst out of the car. She ran across the tarmac towards them with Lupi, Drake, and me in hot pursuit. She stopped in front of the crowd and flapped her arms wildly.

"Hey, there, I know you've all been waiting for me, so here I am!" she yelled. Then she broke into song.

People gasped.

"What is *that*?" someone cried.

As soon as we caught her up, Lupi and Drake took her by the arms and started to lead her away. "Look, Antonia, they weren't expecting you. And they don't understand you," Drake whispered gently.

"I'm making myself perfectly clear," she insisted. "And besides, some of them look delicious."

With great effort the three of us managed to drag her backstage and hide her in an empty dressing room. After changing into our costumes, we went back to see how she was doing.

She had pulled all the clothes off the hangers and drapped them over her head and arms. "How do I look?" she asked, cackling.

At that moment Monica passed the dressing room door, stopping to stare at Antonia in horror. "Samantha! Where do you find these people? How horrible!"

"I wonder if she tastes any better than she looks," hissed Antonia.

I squelched a giggle. Dr and Mr Brown offered to take Antonia into the audience to sit with them. I felt relieved to get rid of her.

When Tommy and Iris arrived, we selected the instruments we were going to play for our first number. Iris would play the jaws harp with Drake on the flute, Tommy on guitar, me on the piano, and Lupi and Iris singing. Lupi planned on using a kettledrum, a tortoiseshell drum, a scraper, and a rattle to produce some backgroud noises.

When the audience quietened down, we started to play, easing in with the odd haunting sound of the flute, followed by various drumbeats and other sounds. It all blended together niecly, producing an African-flavoured mix. We played three more songs and sounded really good. The crowd loved the music.

Halfway through the last song, I heard Antonia screeching. People started to turn around, trying to see where the noise was coming from. Iris looked questioningly at me, but I shrugged. What could I tell her?

Suddenly we saw Antonia rise from her seat

and flap her arms, still shrieking. By this time, everyone was staring at her, not paying any attention to us. She stepped over people, scrambling over the seats as if she were searching for something, then grabbed a member of the audience as though she'd picked him out specially. The man quickly freed himself from her grasp and started running.

"It's trying to bite me!" he cried.

Dr and Mr Brown raced after Antonia and grabbed her just in time. But she wriggled away from them and clambered up onto the stage with us. When Iris saw Antonia baring her long fangs, she screamed, dropping the jaws harp to the floor. Lupi and Drake tackled Antonia, holding her back. Tommy tried to keep playing the guitar, but everbody else had stopped playing their instruments. Our whole song fell apart. When we stopped, the room was buzzing with excitement.

"Antonia, Iris is our friend. Please be nice to her," Lupi pleaded.

"What? You guys actually *know* this thing?" cried Iris. "I can't believe it! On second thought, after everything that's happened, I *can* believe it!"

"Samantha, who is she?" Tommy wanted to know.

"Lupi and Drake's cousin, their music teacher," I explained, forcing a laugh. "You can't take her anywhere."

The stage manager hurried over to us. "Look, you'll have to get her out of here or leave," he said quietly but firmly. "People are threatening to call the police. I don't want to be forced to do that, but she's disturbing the peace."

He turned to leave, but Iris ran after him. "What about the contest?" she demanded.

"Look, if you get her out of here now, if you're lucky, people might forget about her. But I can't make any promises about whether the Battle of the Bands will be able to keep you on."

"What?" we chorused.

"This will look terrible on our performance record," Tommy moaned.

"We've done really well up until now," I reminded him.

"Well, I've had enough, Samantha." Iris glared at me. "We've had some sort of problem with every performance. And after this, I'll bet we never get to perform in the Battle of the Bands again, let alone win. I'm doing the only thing I can do — I'm quitting!"

"Iris!" I cried, grabbing her sleeve. She shrugged me off, but Tommy and I followed her backstage. "You can't quit. We need you!"

"Yes, I can," she shouted. "I'm tired of being scared to death, and I'm tired of all the interruptions. This is no way to get famous — by being a freak show. Not unless you want a career with the circus."

"Iris!" I exclaimed.

"I'm not putting up with this any more, Sam. I don't think this is any way to run a rock band." She grabbed her things and stomped off.

"You know, she's right about some of that," Tommy admitted.

"Whose side are you on, Tommy?" I

demanded. "My friends are not a freak show. They just happen to be very strange. And you already knew that before you got into this."

"But I didn't know *how* weird they were," he objected. "I didn't know one of their relatives would try biting people, for instance. That's a little hard to take."

"That wasn't supposed to happen," I insisted. "Antonia wasn't even supposed to come here."

"She acts like . . . a vampire," he said, laughing at his own words.

"I can't believe you and Iris can just leave the group at a time like this! Just because things get a little tough!" Furious, I left him standing there and went to find Lupi and Drake.

"We took Antonia out to the car," Drake told me. "Is everything all right?"

"No, but we'll manage." I sighed. "Come on, let's go home."

We packed up our instruments and walked outside. But just as we rounded the corner of the building, I turned around and realized Drake was no longer with us. Lupi and I went back to look for him. We found him outside the stage door, talking to that short man again.

"That's one of the two men who have been buying Drake's potions," I told Lupi.

Drake dug into his pocket for something and handed the stranger a big bottle of yellow powder that looked like the stuff he had used at the mall.

"Now just sprinkle on paper or rocks," Drake instructed. "And almost right away, it will turn into money."

"Just a minute here," I cried out, rushing towards them. "Drake, I told you not to do this again without asking me first."

"But I had to, Samantha," he insisted. "You keep saying no. I only need to sell one more spell after this one, and we can but that video camera."

The stranger thrust an envelope at Drake, but I ordered him to hand it back. "I told you before, you can't take money for this! Look, I'll ask my parents to rent a video camera for us so we can tape the last performance. We can afford that."

Times were certainly easier before the kids became aware of money, I thought. The stranger just shrugged when I stuffed the envelope back in his pocket.

"We don't need your money, whoever you are!" I yelled, glaring at him.

"His name is Nick," Drake told me.

Nick forced a smile and walked away — with the money potion tucked securely under his arm.

I started to go after him, but Drake held me back.

"How much money can he make with that potion?" I demanded.

Drake shrugged. "Lots, but what difference does it make? He can't keep the money forever."

"What do you mean?"

"Don't you remember? I told you, it dissolves after a little while," Drake replied simply.

Somehow I'd forgotten that piece of

information. "I wonder what will happen when Nick and Hester find that out," I said.

Chapter 10

I WAS STANDING on the lunch line at school on Monday when Monica Hammond breezed over. She looked as though she couldn't wait to talk to me.

"Samantha, what happened to your band the other day?" she oozed. "After you got kicked out, did Blood break up?"

"Sort of," I answered defiantly. "Iris quit, but that doesn't mean the band broke up."

Her eyebrows popped up. "Oh, is that all? I thought you had been kicked out of the competition, too. After that weirdo messed up your act on Friday, how can you face another audience?"

"Next!" the person behind the counter called. I welcomed the interruption and made my order extra long in the hopes that we wouldn't have to continue our conversation. After I got my food, I left Monica standing there.

I'd made the situation sound better than it was. I definitely had problems. Iris had quit, Tommy and I were mad at each other, the Battle of the Bands manager was annoyed with us, and Drake was selling potions to a lunatic. Things couldn't be much worse, I decided.

I bumped into Maurice as I was threading my way through the cafeteria tables.

"Hey, Samanatha, I loved your vampire act. A bunch of us wanted to tell the band people that they should definitely keep you guys on. You're the best," he gushed.

"Really?" I squeaked in surprise. "Oh, boy, is that great to hear, Maurice."

Just as I got home from school that day, the phone rang. But the caller didn't talk, just breathed.

"Who is it? Who is it?" I demanded.

"Stay out of the Browns' lives, if you know what's good for you," a mysterious, muffled voice warned. The caller sounded as if he had socks stuffed in his mouth.

"Tell me who you are," I insisted, but he hung up. I wondered whether it was the shadowy Nick or the lunatic Mark Hester. This was getting scary.

I thought about going to the police, but I realized I didn't really have any evidence of anything. And besides, who would believe that one of the county's candidates was threatening a babysitter because he wanted magic potions from an eight-year-old boy?

When I babysat for the Browns later that evening, Lupi and Drake seemed unusually happy to see me.

"Samanatha, we thought you might not come," Lupi exclaimed, hugging my waist.

"Why would you think that?" I asked. "Haven't I always come when I said I would?"

"Because of what Monica said," Drake sniffled, almost close to tears.

"Monica talked to you?"

"Yes. She called us to say that if Blood became famous, then you wouldn't need to babysit us anymore, and we would never see you," he explained. "We were frightened."

It took a lot to frighten Lupi and Drake. I hugged them both. "That's not true! If Blood became famous, I'd still babysit you. And besides, we'd spend more time together because we'd be rehearsing, too."

Lupi looked at her brother in delight. "That's right. Why didn't we think of that?"

"Come on. Let's turn on the TV and see how my potion worked," Drake said gleefully.

A local station was televising a live speech by each candidate at the end of its regular news broadcast. We watched the other candidates who gave normal political speeches, promising to make the county a better place to live in.

"And now we present Mark Hester, candidate for supervisor," the moderator announced.

Mark Hester strode up to the podium and smiled. He had dressed nicely — almost normally — as though he'd gone out and bought all new clothes.

"Ladies and gentlemen, I have great news for you. Your city and county tax dollars will be returned to you — in full. It's a promise I can make, because I have the power to return your money."

A loud murmur travelled through the assembled crowd. The camera skimmed over the excited audience.

"I know that some of you feel you pay too much in taxes, that you've been ripped off. You feel that the county takes a lot and gives little in return. But trust me, that's all going to change. We now have the money we need to make the changes that need to be made."

He rubbed his chin, and then he began to sing in rhyme, I realized he had rubbed on some of Drake's potion.

"We can build a great county, with our increased bounty. . . . "

Another ripple of excitement rose from the crowd and the camera caught Nick passing out leaflets. Hester continued speaking, looking very pleased with himself. "You'll do great with Hester, 'cause he's no jester. For the county he'll make money, and turn molasses to honey."

"I didn't give him a potion that can do that," Drake objected.

"I think he's getting carried away," I explained. "I think he thinks he can do anything now."

"You might say it's a trick," Hester went on. The camera followed his every movement. "But it's a trick in your favour, as you will see. A candidate with a philanthropic bent, you'd have to consider heaven-sent. And that is me, I kid you not, I am here to improve your lot. Life will be better, and you can bet, that all your civic needs will be met, when you vote for Hester, who is the best."

By this time the crowd was clapping and cheering for Hester, waving their leaflets in the air. "We want Hester, we want Hester!" they chanted in unison.

The scene sent chills through me. Hester was in his glory, waving at the excited crowd.

He had finished his speech, but the announcer picked up where Hester left off. "Mark Hester, a dark horse candidate just two weeks ago, is definitely in the running now. The latest polls put him right up there with the other popular candidates. Unnamed sources have revealed that Hester plans to make a substantial contribution to the Mirot Dental Clinic, which provides free dental care to needy children. And Hester has changed his tune about the proposed convention centre at Jones Park, maintaining that the park should be preserved and pledging to donate his own money to build more recreational facilities there. But a worrisome question hangs in everyone's minds. Where has Hester found the kind of money to conduct this kind of campaign?"

"Only we know the answer to that," I said.

Candidates for other offices presented speeches then, but you could tell they were all a little worried. I don't think they ever expected to have Hester as a real competitor.

About an hour after the broadcast the phone rang. Drake answered it, when he motioned to Lupi and me, we scrunched into the phone booth to listen.

It was Nick. "Hester wants a lot more of the money-making potion. He'll pay double for it, but he needs you to start working on it now, because he wants it as soon as possib—"

We heard a scuffle over the phone, then someone shouting, "Give me that phone!"

Hester got on the phone. "Drake? Are you there? I want you to understand how important this is. This is the big time now, kid. I want a lot of the money-making potion so we can really change these people's minds about me. I'm not just thinking of becoming county supervisor now. That's small potatoes, boy. Just a stepping stone." He cackled madly for a full minute. "After I become supervisor, I'm running for governor."

We all looked at each other solemnly. Drake exchanged a few words with Hester before hanging up the phone.

"What are we going to do?" I exclaimed.

Chapter 11

I FELT THAT I should stick close to the Brown kids whenever possible, so I started going over to their house every night of the week. I'd also been hoping to hear whether or not we would be able to continue performing in the Battle of the Bands, but no one had called about it and I couldn't seem to reach Mr Spenck, the contest organizer, on the phone. I was getting discouraged.

I was at the Browns' house on Wednesday when Hester called. He was furious. Drake held the phone away from his ear so that we could all hear Hester screaming.

"Your money disappeared! What kind of bogus potion is this anyway? It just vanished into thin air! My bank claims that they placed my big deposit in a safe deposit box, but when they went back to count it, it was gone! They say they can't cover my cheque to the Mirot Dental Clinic! Or to the Parks Department! People are going to turn against me! You've got to stop them!" he ranted.

"What if I don't want to?" Drake asked.

"Let's just say that I would hate to see

anything bad happen to you, young man," Hester warned, his voice low and menacing.

Lupi and I exchanged worried looks and I wrapped a comforting arm around Drake's thin shoulders.

"This time I want a potion that will make them love me, make them vote only for me. I call it Operation Mind Change and I've got it all planned out. Here's how it will work. I'll hire an aeroplane to drop the potion over the whole population of the county. Suddenly they'll see everything differently. They won't be able to think of anything else, only that they want Mark Hester as county supervisor." He giggled maniacally, obviously pleased with his plan. "It will have to be a long-lasting potion, something that will work at least until the election. And then, when I run for governor next term, we'll use the potion again, only we'll do it to the entire state!"

The three of us had pressed close together while listening to Hester's tirade. If only the public knew what he was really like!

"I want you to bring the potion to me tomorrow evening at the benefit dinner for the Dental Clinic where I'll be speaking." He supplied directions and the address. "And keep that pesky babysitter out of this, kid."

Drake didn't answer; he just hung up the phone.

We all hugged each other for a few minutes.

Drake sighed. "Well, I'd better get to work on those potions. Don't worry, Samanatha, I've got an idea."

"I have to worry, Drake," I cried. "Mark

Hester just threatened you if you didn't produce the potion!"

"But he won't know what he's getting," he replied. He walked slowly down the hall to his laboratory and closed the door.

On Thursday, Lupi, Drake, and I took a bus down to the Mirot Dental Clinic. Hester had told Drake to meet him in a room adjacent to the main hall, where he was scheduled to deliver his speech. Posters depicting a big tooth hung from all the doors; all the information about the Clinic was printed across the tooth. While Drake went inside the room, Lupi and I situated ourselves behind a big rubber plant in the hallway, which afforded us a view of almost half of the room.

We could clearly see Mark Hester was furious about something. He ripped off his tie and flung it across the room. He stormed around the room in a rage, occasionally slipping out of our view. I couldn't see Drake at all. Hester suddenly grabbed Nick around the neck as though he were going to strangle him. Nick struggled to free himself from Hester's grasp, but he couldn't seem to get away from him. They were shouting at each other, but I couldn't understand what either person was saying.

Then Drake stepped into my view. He handed Hester three huge mayonnaise jars full of some grainy brown stuff.

Neither Lupi nor I knew what the new potion would do. We only knew that it would affect the entire county. All we could do was wait and see.

After Drake emerged from the room, we all decided to hang around so we could listen to Hester's speech. As soon as he came into sight his audience began to boo him.

The candidate climbed to the podium, held up his arms for silence, and smiled with forced patience at the crowd. "Friends, I think I owe you an explanation. Although you may have heard rumours that my money is no good, I'm here to assure you that it's not true. My bank simply miscounted it. I am true to my word, and as I promised, every unjust tax dollar that you have paid out will be returned to you. Don't fear, my friends, your money will soon be back in your pockets."

He stepped down from the podium and started to approach the audience. But they angrily rose to meet him, throwing their dinner napkins and leaflets in his face and brandishing knives and forks. TV cameras zoomed in on the stricken candidate and the furious crowd.

Just then, Hester spotted me and lunged forward through the crowd, but his aides dragged him back.

"Let's get out of here!" I cried, taking Lupi's and Drake's hands. We ran out to the street and hopped on a bus just as it started to pull away from the curb.

My heart was pounding as I sat down. I suddenly realized that being afraid of what Hester might do had taken over our whole lives. But I had other responsibilities, too. I still had to work on getting our band back together. I remembered what Maurice Maklowitz had said to me about Blood. People liked to be scared —

entertainment scared, that is, not life-or-death scared. They screamed first and enjoyed it later.

We only had a couple of days left until our last concert — if we performed at all. I'd been so depressed about my friends and the group — but maybe I had no reason to be. Maybe we could patch things up and go ahead. Just because we had had one failure, it didn't mean we were washed up for good.

By the time we got back to the Browns', it was almost nine o'clock, but I decided to call Mr Spenck one more time. "Hey, I was wondering if you might consider letting Blood perform in the Battle of the Bands again," I said haltingly.

"Consider it? You mean nobody's called to tell you?"

"Uh, no," I gulped, expecting the worst.

"Hey, you guys might be a lot of trouble," Mr Spenck admitted, "but people love your group. A lot of kids wrote saying they wanted to hear more of you, so as far as I'm concerned, you're on."

As soon as I hung up, I called Tommy. "We have to get our group together and rehearse," I told him.

"What about Iris?" he asked. "She quit, remember?"

"Don't worry, I'm going to try and convince her. Look, we didn't have any trouble until our last performance, and that won't happen again. We can make sure Antonia doesn't come. I already spoke to Mr Spenck, and he said people really liked the group even though we were scary." I told him my theory about the way people liked to be scared and then laugh afterwards.

"Okay, say no more. Count me in. And uh" — he cleared his throat — "I'm sorry about the way I acted and everything."

"Listen, I'm sorry for how I acted, too," I confessed. "You were right about Antonia. She is a real problem."

I felt warm all over and more confident than ever knowing that he was with us again.

Iris wasn't as easy to convince, however. I stopped at her house on the way home to ask her to rejoin the band.

"Look, Sam, I meant what I said. I quit the band." She offered me a Coke. "I think your friendship with the Browns has gone too far. How can you be sure they won't bring something worse next time?"

"They won't, Iris, I promise. Just come back to the band. I talked to Mr Spenck earlier tonight and he told me people liked the craziness. They want us back. They really liked being scared — just the way they like horror movies."

"Look, this isn't a horror movie," she insisted. "A horror movie is all sets and makeup. You can turn off the TV if you don't like it. But you can't turn off the Brown family. And you can't even know what will happen the next time we perform. So how can you even decide whether you want to be part of it or not?"

"But don't you see? That's part of the appeal. Our band is a hundred times better than a horror movie because you don't know what to expect. And you know how popular horror movies are. People love them, just the way they love Blood."

"We're a living horror movie," she groaned.

"Come on, give it another try," I urged. "We really need you."

She sighed heavily. "I know I'll regret this, but I'll regret it even more if you guys become a big success without me."

I hugged her. "You won't regret it, Iris. We'll be the best rock band ever."

She rolled her eyes. I quickly called Tommy and the Browns, and we arranged a quick rehearsal for the next day.

Friday after school we all gathered at Tommy's house. Lupi and Drake seemed especially happy to be there.

"I have an idea. We can eat the instruments at the end of our act," said Drake, pretending to chomp down on a flute.

Iris frowned. "That could be dangerous. I don't think they're very digestable."

"I think we should be as exciting as we can be!" cried Lupi. "Maybe we can dress up as drops of blood."

Iris shuddered. "Monica's talking about having all kinds of stage props in her performance. You'd think she was in a Broadway production or something."

"I've seen her posters around school," Tommy added. "But we can make posters, too."

"Well, we'd better get to work," I urged. "We only have a day before the big concert."

"Remember you said you'd ask your parents

to rent a video recorder?" Drake asked.

"I will," I promised.

We played a couple of our best songs, then attempted the harder ones. Lupi and Drake were on their best behaviour. They must have guessed that Iris couldn't take too much more excitement from them.

After the rehearsal we all walked out of Tommy's house together.

Monica, riding her bike past the house, braked suddenly and squinted at us. "I don't believe my eyes. You guys are back together?"

"That right," Lupi cried happily.

"We'll be performing at the concert tomorrow night, so watch out," I warned.

"Boy, this is news," Monica huffed. "I thought you guys were completely out. I mean, after that last scene, how could you possibly show your faces in public again?"

"Easy," answered Iris. "We're a sensation. Hey, maybe we should call ourselves The Sensations."

"I don't think you guys stand a chance," Monica said.

"We're not afraid to find out." Tommy grinned at her.

"Ha!" she cried , pedalling away.

The drone of a small aeroplane buzzed overhead. Tommy, Iris, and I looked up and noticed something brown speckling the sky, falling from the back of the plane.

"What is that stuff?" Tommy asked. "Do you think they're dumping hazardous waste from the sky now?"

Iris laughed. "You should write an article

about it, Tommy: 'Hazardous Waste Distributed Evenly Over County'."

In the distance I saw another plane — just over the central part of Plainview.

Within minutes we all started to sneeze. We couldn't stop sneezing.

"It worked!" Drake cried triumphantly.

"What worked?" Tommy and Iris chorused.

Drake was sneezing so violently that he couldn't tell them.

"What's he talking about, Samantha?" Tommy asked.

I didn't want to say anything in front of Iris, so I just shrugged. "Beats me." Then I sneezed, too.

We said good-bye to Tommy. After we walked Iris home, I dropped the kids off at their house and then went home myself.

The phone was ringing when I walked into the empty house.

"Hello?" I answered, out of breath.

The person on the other end sneezed. It was our man with the disguised voice. "I'm telling you one more time. Stay away from the Browns. I want Drake, and I want you to stay away from him, or else something terrible will happen to all of you."

"Is this a threat?" I asked the obvious. It certainly wasn't a party invitation.

He didn't answer.

"Who are you, anyway?" I cried desperately.

"None of your business," he answered gruffily.

"I'm calling the police," I threatened, stifling a sneeze.

"You'd better not," he warned in a cold tone. Then he hung up.

The dial tone buzzed monotonously in my ear. I looked around me, scanning the room for some sign of disruption, some sign of a stranger in my life. But everything looked the same. He had really scared me this time — I was convinced that he could be extremely dangerous.

And what had he said? He wanted Drake, and he wanted me out of the way. I remembered the way Mark Hester had reacted when he spotted me in the Dental Clinc. Sneezing, my hands shaking, I dialled the police.

"I want to report a threatening phone call." My voice trembled. "Someone is threatening me and the kids I babysit."

"Do you have any idea who the caller might be?" the police officer asked.

"I have a pretty good idea."

"What exactly did the caller threaten?"

"Well, this time he claimed something terrible would happen if I didn't stay away from the kids, and the last time, the boy I babysit for was told that if he didn't make this magic potion, something bad might happen to him."

"Magic potion? Come on, be serious," the desk officer scoffed.

"Look, never mind the reasons. We've been threatened, that's all. I think we need protection." I knew that if I mentioned Mark Hester, the police officer wouldn't believe me at all.

"If you'll give us the authorization, we can try to put a tracer on him," the officer explained, punctuating his words with sneezes. "But you'll have to try and keep him on the line next time he calls. Other than that, the best I can do is increase your neighbourhood patrols. We'll just have to wait until something happens."

"Why wait until something happens? One of us could be . . . dead!" I cried dramatically.

"I'm sorry, young lady, but that's how the law works," he told me. "We need to have some proof that a crime has been committed."

I thanked him for increasing the police patrol, gave him our names and addresses, and hung up. Then I sank down in a leather chair in the dark study and thought about everything that had happened. Until that moment, I had thought the Browns were the scariest thing that had ever happened to me. But I wasn't so sure any more.

Chapter 12

"AS I'M SURE everyone here this Saturday night to witness the final Battle of the Bands already knows, tonight's performance will determine who the winning band is," the announcer explained, between sneezes, to hundreds of fans. "Even if your favourite doesn't get chosen as the winner tonight there's a good chance for a band to be discovered here — especially this year with such a talented turnout of young artists." With that, the announcer buried his nose in a handkerchief.

Backstage, the five of us clapped and sneezed nervously. I hadn't let Drake and Lupi out of my sight for a second since we'd arrived at the concert hall, for fear that something might happen to them. Drake didn't seem very afraid when I told him about the caller, but then I think he's much braver than me in general. He'd have to be to live the life he lives.

Drake had assured me that the sneeze potion would wear off eventually, but in the meantime we still had to sing. We were all sneezing so much that Drake had even developed an antisneeze formula — a lime-green powder that he dusted all around the inside of the stage, dressing rooms, and auditorium.

Drake sprinkled the rest of the antisneeze potion backstage while the announcer continued his introduction. Then I left both Lupi and Drake in Tommy's and Iris' care while I went to my dressing room. As I switched on the light, something flew through the air. I clutched at the big blue blob that had plonked onto my upper arm, but it didn't want to come off. It felt like a blob of jam, but when I tried to remove it, it grew hard and attached itself to my skin. I was still wrestling with the blob when Lupi and Drake ran in.

"Oh, Samantha, we were just coming to tell you about our blobs," Drake said apologetically. "They get attached to people so easily."

"Drake, I thought I told you not to bring anything weird here," I reminded him.

Drake grabbed the blob with both hands and peeled it off my skin.

"Ouch!" I cried. "It feels like you're peeling off a bandage."

"I'm not crazy about blobs, as you know," Lupi admitted, "but they're interesting to other people. And when we heard that Monica was going all out to win the competition, we decided we needed something really special." Drake showed me a burlap bag like the one he had used to transport Lawrence the boa. When he yanked open the drawstring, I saw a chalkboard, packages of fake fingernails, a bucket, and some yellow, red, and blue blobs — just like the one that had attacked me.

"What are you planning to do with all that stuff?" I asked.

"You'll see," Drake replied mysteriously.

"Just don't do anything to make Iris hysterical," I warned. "Remember, we want to win."

"I'm here! I'm here!" cried a small voice. Kimmie ran towards us and hurled herself into my arms.

"Hi — what are you doing back here?" I asked.

"I'm helping with the special effects," she crowed. "Right, Lupi?"

"We have it all planned." Lupi nodded and led her to the stage, while Drake and I went to get a ladder from one of the lighting people.

Drake set up the ladder behind the curtains. He took the bucket out of the bag and half-filled it with water, then attached it to a rope on a pulley that hung down next to the ladder. He set up the little chalkboard at the base of the ladder and handed Kimmie the fake fingernails.

Our scenery consisted of a series of panels that the Browns had hand-painted. All done up in blacks, browns, and dark green, it made you think of the evil forest in *The Wizard of Oz*.

"Don't you think you should've asked the rest of us if this would be okay?" I asked.

"We didn't want to — we thought you'd say no to everything," Lupi replied.

"I never say no to everything," I protested.

The three kids giggled.

"What's all this stuff for?" Tommy asked, coming up behind us to see what was going on.

"The fake fingernails are for Kimmie to drag

along the chalkboard," Drake explained.
"She's going to slosh the water for some more
sound effects. Then we have some blobs we'll
use on the scenery."

"Blobs?" Tommy questioned.

At that moment the announcer's voice
boomed at us: "And now, one of our favourite
bands . . . the spectacular Spectaculars!"

Applause filled the room as Monica and her
feathered friends strutted onto the stage in all
their glory. They all climbed onto a huge
cardboard boat, painted the same colours as
their feathers — bright blues, greens, and
purples.

Monica's voice rose pure and clear above the
others, and I wished for a moment that I could
sing like that. She really was good, and so were
the other Spectaculars. They harmonized
perfectly and played their instruments
beautifully, too.

Suddenly, during the The Spectaculars' last
number, Monica's arm shot up to feel her
feathers. I thought it was just part of her act, but
then a flood of water poured down on top of her,
drenching her. The audience burst into
laughter, but the band kept playing.

I turned towards Kimmie and ran over to see
what had happened. Straining to get a better
look at the stage, she had moved closer and
closer to the stage, pulling the bucket of water
higher and higher up into the rafters. When it
had finally reached the pulley, the bucket had
tipped over from the force of her action.

"Kimmie, you just dumped water all over
Monica!" I cried.

She giggled.

The music stopped and everyone applauded.

"I heard that!" Monica stormed up behind me. "And I'm going to tell the Battle of the Bands manager to kick you out of the competition!"

Wet feathers clung to her skin and hair. "Monica, it was an accident," I explained. "You can't have us kicked out!"

"I'll do everything I can, Samantha," she retorted. "You've been nothing but trouble. Scaring people, messing up my performance." Her wet feathers drooping limply around her angry face, she whirled around and stomped away.

A few minutes later Monica returned with two of the organizers of the Battle of the Bands. She pointed at me and Kimmie. "They're the ones who had me drenched."

"Did you intentionally get Monica wet?" asked Ms Malkey, one of the organizers.

"Of course not," I declared. "It was an accident. Kimmie was setting up something for our performance. She didn't spill the water on purpose."

"Don't believe a word she says," Monica insisted. "I want them out of the competition."

"Look, we did have trouble with your band at the last performance," Ms Malkey admitted. "You pretty much had the place cleared out with that weirdo you brought in here. However, I also realize that Monica has a stake in getting you out of the competition because you're so good."

"That's not true," Monica cried. "We're

better than they are. I'm not afraid of any competition."

Ms Malkey nodded as though she were only half listening.

In the background I could hear the din of the crowd, but I had no idea why they were making so much noise. I figured they were still responding to the Spectaculars' great performance.

Ms Malkey and the other organizer turned their attention to the crowd. The other one, a young, short-haired woman, went out front to see what all the commotion was.

Ms Malkey cleared her throat noisily. "Okay, no more trouble then. I'll talk to the judges and explain that what happened to Monica was an accident."

The other organizer returned, smiling. "It looks like the fans out there are screaming for Blood," she joked, wincing as she said it. "You guys better get out there."

Monica turned beet-red and glared at me. "I swear, Samantha, you haven't heard the last of me."

"I'm sure I haven't," I replied, grinning.

As I ran back to join the others, I heard the emcee announce us. "And now, let's hear it for the very funny, strange, and popular band that you heard first right here at the Battle of the Bands — here they are . . . Blood!"

Iris grabbed her spoons. "Come on. Let's knock 'em dead."

Tommy and I went first, holding our arms up in the air like champions. The crowd went wild. The stage crew had already put our scenery in place and Kimmie dropped a few of the blobs onto it. I gazed out into the audience, searching for my parents. I spotted my mother in the aisle, holding the rented video recorder. I smiled at her and sat down at the piano.

First we sang "The Scare Song", as the kids liked to call it. Kimmie scraped the fake fingernails over the blackboard, and Iris played the spoons. Tommy came in on the guitar. Lupi started singing and then Iris joined her. It sounded perfect — like nothing you ever heard before.

People began to clap when they saw the multicoloured blobs sliding down the face of the scenery.

We launched into another song, one that only Iris sang, which everyone loved. Then we did two more featuring Kimmie's sound effects. After our fourth song Drake ran offstage for a minute and returned looking very mysterious. I was wondering what he had done when the sound of thousands of hissing snakes filled the room, followed by my screams.

"Is that you, Samantha?" Tommy asked.

"Uh, I guess so. It's a long story." I gulped, feeling my face grow hot. I turned to Drake. "You didn't tell me you were going to use this tonight."

"It's the perfect time." Drake grinned mischievously.

"Come on. Let's play 'Hug Me' with the hissing as background," suggested Tommy.

Actually "Hug Me" was a terrific song idea. The song had little empty pockets in it that the hissing and screaming filled. The audience stood up and clapped wildly at the end. They demanded an encore, and even after we gave them one, they still wanted more. We were allowed to do one more song, but then we had to give up the stage to the next band.

Drake ran ahead of us as we left the stage, eager to retrieve his snake tape. I figured he'd be okay, but when I came out of the dressing room less than a minute later, I couldn't find him.

"Have you seen Drake?" I asked the others.

"Not since we came offstage," answered Tommy.

"We'd better look for him," I decided. Iris, Kimmie, Tommy, Lupi, and I split up, searching in all the dressing rooms and behind the curtains. Just as I peered behind a long curtain in a far corner of the backstage area, a hand reached out and grabbed me.

In that terrifying split second I saw my two friends — Tommy and Lupi — gagged with bright scraps of material, their hands forced behind their backs. Our captors wore stocking masks so that we couldn't recognize them, but I could tell by their outfits that both of them were men. Each of us tried to fight back, but they were much stronger and quicker than we were. The three of us looked at one another helplessly.

Then one of the men wrapped fabric around my eyes and everything went black. I felt myself being dragged away and heard the scuff-scuff of my friends' shoes as they were dragged away, too. I was pushed, like a sack of potatoes, onto a hard metal floor, and I heard an engine come to life. Then I knew that they were driving us away from the concert.

My biggest fears had come true. We were being kidnapped!

Chapter 13

AFTER OUR RIDE we were hustled to our feet and pushed through an open door. The building smelled of Sheetrock, wood shavings, and metal, so I guessed that some kind of construction was going on there. Then we were pushed through another doorway.

Someone in the room groaned and one of our captors snapped, "Shut up, kid."

I guessed that the groaner must be Drake. Despite our predicament, I felt relieved to find him. Our captors roughly sat us down on some chairs, sneezed loudly, and walked out the door, closing it behind them.

A minute later the door opened again with a loud bang.

"The boy's over there," a man growled — it was Nick, I was sure! Except this time he hadn't bothered to disguise his voice at all, and he was sneezing a lot. And then the pieces of the puzzle began to slide into their rightful places. Nick's was the threatening voice I'd heard over the phone. It wasn't Hester's voice or anyone else's.

The other one — Mark Hester, I was sure — walked across the floor. "Hey, kid. We can't make heads or tails of that bag of yours," Hester complained. "You'll have to come with us. I need your help to win this election."

I groaned loudly in protest.

"Oh, shut up," Hester snarled. "The rest of you will have to wait and see how your friend does. We don't trust him to do what we want anymore, so we're holding all of you until after the election on Tuesday. That way we know he'll do what we want. Your little friend here is going to create a potion that will destroy the other candidates' political careers. I'm convinced Drake has something like that in his bag of tricks. I want to see the other candidates embarrass themselves, expose themselves as idiots."

"We'll keep you locked up safely until Hester has won the election. After he's in power, no one will ever believe your story. It'll be the word of a bunch of kids against that of the county supervisor. So make yourselves comfortable," Nick invited us with a laugh.

"I'm very tired of your pranks, Drake," Hester added with a snarl. "Just keep that in mind."

I wanted to scream — the thought of being stuck with these crazy people until after the election, even though it was only two days away, was too awful. We had to get out of here somehow!

I heard growling: Lupi! Her strong musky animal scent filled my nostrils. I hoped the kidnappers wouldn't see her during the change. I could tell Tommy was trying to say something, but I couldn't understand him.

I heard the kidnappers drag Drake out of the room, slamming the door behind them. Poor Drake! I was certain he didn't have anything in his bag that could destroy people politically. He *could* make things difficult, but I didn't think he would do that in this case.

Lupi growled deep in her throat. I heard her thrashing around, tearing at the ropes with her teeth and shredding the fabric, then her clear, unmuffled growl. You could sense that an animal was in the room. I think she forgot about us because she padded in the direction of the door. Tommy and I shouted through our gagged mouths. Of course, it didn't occur to me until later that Tommy was shouting because he heard a wild animal in the room with us. Lupi could be scary, but I had got used to her. She let out a yelp and padded over to us.

She bit through my ropes first. But when she tore away the blindfold from Tommy's eyes, he gasped. He was looking at a full-fledged, real live werewolf smiling down at him. In fact, the more he stared at her, the more he looked as if he was in shock.

"Tommy, it's okay, really," I comforted him. "I know exactly what you're thinking. Lupi does turn into a werewolf sometimes, but it's usually nothing to be afraid of. In fact, in this case it will be a blessing."

A loud croak came from Tommy's mouth, but he still couldn't talk.

"Tommy, if you make any noise, I'm going to have to gag you again so they won't hear us," I told him gently.

"Who — who is that?" he managed to ask.

"Did you say *Lupi*?"

"It *is* Lupi," I assured him. "She's normal most of the time, as you know, but she has her moments. Don't worry though. You've seen her this way before and nothing happened. Remember the Halloween party?"

He slapped his face as though he were trying to wake up from a bad dream. "I saw her this way at school during your campaign," he remembered. "But I always thought she was wearing a c-costume!"

"Yeah, so did I when I first met her," I confessed. "Everybody does . . . unless you've been there when she changed." I took his hand. "Come on. We have to get out of here."

We looked around the room. Stacks of boards occupied one corner, topped by layers of Sheetrock. The wooden floor was covered with some carpet remnants. With no windows in the room, we had no way of knowing where we were.

"Maybe we're in a warehouse," Tommy suggested.

Lupi went to work on the lock on the door, the kind that you usually open by inserting the key into the doorknob. But Lupi just cranked the knob hard and broke the lock.

We crept outside the room and glanced around, letting Lupi go first. We checked every single room of the building, an old inn in the process of being renovated, but there was no one in sight.

"They must have left with him already," Lupi growled. "Look at the footprints." She knelt down and traced two sets of shoe prints plus the double furrow made by the heels of somebody's being half carried. Moving outside, we saw tyre tracks in the soft sand of the parking area, but we couldn't see a single car or truck.

"They took him away, but I'll bet they're headed for the debate," I guessed. "That way they can make Drake try his potions out right on the spot."

"But nobody — not even Drake — ever knows what his potions will turn out like," Lupi snarled in her deep growly voice.

"Wow, that voice is wild," Tommy sounded surprised. "I guess we should get ourselves to the debate then. City Hall, right?"

"Right," I answered, glad that Tommy and I were up on our current events. "But first, we should call the police."

"What will you tell them?" Lupi wanted to know.

I ducked into one of the pay phones in the lobby of the inn and inserted a quarter. "I'll tell them just enough to get them to help," I confided. "Hello, yes, I'm calling to report a kidnapping. Yes. An eight-year-old boy. I saw — well, I *heard* him being kidnapped. He'll be at City Hall really soon."

"They're holding a live television debate at City Hall tonight, young lady," the desk officer told me gruffly.

"I know that, but you have to listen to me. Go there and look for the boy. I also know that this has something to do with Mark Hester."

"Is this some kind of crank call?" he demanded.

"No, honest, it's for real," I pleaded desperately. "The boy's name is Drake, he has black hair, and he's wearing an old-fashioned suit, a gag, and a blindfold. His hands are tied behind his back." Of course I knew it was unlikely that they would find anyone who fitted that description walking around on the street. I told him my name, where I was calling from, and promised to meet the police at City Hall.

We took a bus to City Hall. The bus driver gave us some strange looks because of the way we were dressed — me in my blood-red dress, Tommy in his antique suit, and worst of all, Lupi as a werewolf.

When we got to City Hall, the police still hadn't arrived. We noticed a few security guards posted in and around the building, and traffic officers on the access roads, but no one else. City Hall was composed of one big hall that looked like a renovated Revolutionary War building. A U-shaped wing of office buildings, built in the same style, jutted out behind it.

We decided to search the office buildings first because we didn't think Hester would want Drake near the site of his TV appearance. We started at one end of the U-shape and worked our way along the building.

Suddenly I noticed a light shining down from a second-floor window. I motioned to the others.

"Look! They're in there!" Tommy whispered.

We watched as Nick leaned against the window above, his broad back blotting out nearly all the light.

"How will we get up there?" Lupi asked. "We can't risk going up and down the staircase."

We surveyed the sheer brick wall, decorated with a climbing vine that clung to a crosshatch of wood.

"I'll climb into the office next door," Lupi offered. "After I make it, you two can follow."

We boosted Lupi onto the crosshatch, which swayed under her weight. She quickly clambered up to the narrow window ledge and peered through the window that framed Nick's back.

"Is Drake in there?" I hissed loudly. She gazed down at us and nodded.

Then she tried the window of the office next door. It wouldn't budge, but she used all of her strength, pulling on the window until the lock broke.

Nick, hearing the sound, turned around and peered outside. Tommy and I ducked down behind a bush as Lupi disappeared into the building and quietly closed the window. Nick opened the window and looked out, but when he didn't see anything unusual, he closed it again and leaned his back against it.

Lupi opened the window of the next office and motioned for us to climb up. I went first, grabbing hold of the slippery vine and pulling myself up. About eight feet off the ground, one of the pieces of wood broke beneath my foot and I started to slide back down the wall, clutching desperately at the vine. But Tommy quickly climbed onto a brick that jutted out from the wall, established a toehold, and stuck his hand under my shoe, stopping my fall. With a small boost from Tommy, I grabbed for the ledge and dragged myself up.

When Tommy took his first step onto the crosshatch, I could see it was ready to collapse. It teetered and shook with each new step.

"Hurry," I whispered urgently. He scooted up the vine-covered structure, reaching the ledge just before the whole wooden support trembled and fell to the ground.

He scrambled through the open window and we all stood silently for a moment, listening for sounds from the next room.

"Maybe if we go out into the hall we'll be able to see into the office," I suggested.

We tiptoed out of the room and into the hallway. We tried to peer through the pane of frosted glass on the door to the next office, but gave up after a minute. We couldn't see anything but shadows.

"It may be a little dangerous, but if one of us went back out onto the ledge, we might be able to find out what's going on in there." I gulped. "Okay, since it was my idea, I'll do it."

I crawled back out the window and perched myself on the ledge, which couldn't have been more than nine inches wide. Trying not to look down, I knelt there waiting for Nick to move out of the way. Finally he leaned forward a little, and I could see Drake looking through his bag. He pulled out a tiny bottle of blue liquid and proceeded to sprinkle drops of the liquid on top of Mark Hester's head. When Drake had finished, Hester stood up to leave.

I moved nearer to the glass, trying to get close

enough to understand their words, but I still couldn't hear what they were saying. I crawled backwards along the ledge and then backed into the room where Lupi and Tommy were waiting. It felt good to have a real floor under my feet again.

"We know they want him to give them something to destroy the other candidates' careers," I said. "But I still don't think he'll give them what they want. And they won't let him go until Hester has won the election. We have to do something!"

"We can't just storm in there and rescue him," Tommy objected. "If they capture us and tie us up again, we won't be of any use to anyone."

"That's true," I agreed. "I think we'll just have to wait for the police to get here. After all, they'll never believe Drake was kidnapped unless they find him in their clutches."

"I hope the police show up soon," growled Lupi.

"I hope the police will show up at all," Tommy said doubtfully.

"Let's go down to the auditorium and watch the debate. That way we can see the police when they arrive, too," I suggested.

When we entered the main auditorium of the City Hall, people studied us with curiosity. A werewolf and two kids dressed in antique clothes were pretty unusual visitors at City Hall.

The room was so crowded, there was hardly even any standing room left. We couldn't see over anyone else's head, so Lupi stood on the arm of a chair and caught a glimpse of the podium.

Mark Hester was angrily pounding his fist on the lectern.

"What are all those police doing here?" somebody in the crowd questioned.

We turned around and saw three bulky police officers crowded in the doorway. They looked as though they meant business.

Tommy, Lupi, and I boldly walked up to them. They looked amused when they saw us.

"We're the ones who made the call," I informed them. "They're holding Drake in an office here — we just saw him. They kidnapped him because Mark Hester wanted Drake to give him a potion. Hester's the one who started all this."

"Mark Hester? A potion? Wait a minute, kid," one of the police officers exclaimed. "What's this potion you're talking about? Are we at a magic show or a debate?"

The others laughed loudly.

"Hester needed the potion to win the election," I explained. "That's why they kidnapped Drake in the first place."

"That's right. They kidnapped him at the Battle of the Bands concert where we're performing," Tommy added.

"A likely story," scoffed a big red-faced police officer.

"But it's all true!" I exclaimed.

"Now I've heard everything," said the third officer, a woman. "Okay, come on. Let's check this report out quickly so we can get back to work."

I asked her to follow me and we led her up to the office where we'd last seen Drake.

Just as we reached the office, Nick opened the door and, pushing Drake in front of him, came face to face with the policewoman.

"Stop right there!" she cried.

Nick shoved — and almost threw — Drake into the police officer's chest, knocking her off her feet, and raced down the hall.

As soon as she caught her breath, the police officer radioed for help. "He's coming your way, Charlie. Down the back stairs. Short — with blond hair and dark glasses."

I ran down the stairs after Nick, caught up with him just outside the door of the building, and grabbed hold of his arm. He tried to shake me off, but I held on tight. At last I saw one of the other police officers running down the walkway towards us. Nick sidestepped him and jumped over a hedge, dragging me along with him, but my weight made him lose his balance. As we fell to the ground, I lost my grip on him and tumbled into the dirt. The policeman dived on top of him, and the two started wrestling. Finally the officer rolled Nick onto his back and handcuffed him.

I ran back upstairs to see how Drake was doing. He blinked in confusion.

"Are you okay?" I asked, patting his cheeks.

"I'm fine," he told me. "Where is everybody?"

"They must have all gone to try to cut Nick off. Or maybe . . . they're going after Hester." I grabbed his hand. "Come on. We have to hurry."

We raced down the stairs and through the deserted hallways. Finally we reached the main auditorium and squeezed through the crowd.

As we pushed towards the stage, we could see Mark Hester screaming his head off, brandishing his fist in the air. "I want to win this election, and I'm powerful enough to do it. You'll *have* to vote for me, all of you!"

Obviously his poetic potion had worn off.

Then Hester spotted Lupi and Tommy, just ahead of me. He pointed at us furiously.

"Get those kids out of here!" he cried wildly. "Stop them!"

Everyone had stopped talking and stared at Hester openmouthed. Children and babies began to cry. Mark Hester, the smiling, hand-shaking politician, suddenly stormed towards us like a crazed animal. When he reached us, Lupi sprang forward, her teeth bared.

Tommy and I held on to her tightly.

"Get him! Get him!" somebody in the crowd yelled. Some others joined in, shouting cries of sympathy for Lupi — amazingly, people were rooting for a werewolf!

"Wait a minute here!" the big red-faced policeman boomed, reaching for Mark Hester. Hester manoeuvered quickly, ducking under the policeman's hands and making a run for the exit. But the police officer grabbed Hester's arm from behind, trying to put him in an arm lock. At that moment, struggling to avoid the police officer's attempts to hold him, Hester punched him right in the nose! The crowd gasped.

"It's that terrible boy who did it!" Mark

Hester screamed. "It's all his fault! He gave me a bad potion!"

A well-dressed woman appeared at Hester's side. "Hush, Mark, you're making a scene," I heard the woman say.

The crowd burst into laughter.

"I've seen and heard a lot of funny things before, Mr Hester, but no kid I know ever *really* made magic potions," the officer said, wagging his head. "And to think I was going to vote for you."

The press went wild, thrusting microphones in Mark Hester's face, snapping pictures. The video cameras rolled. Drake, who had been watching all this intently, suddenly left my side and ran across the stage.

He grinned wildly, yelling, "It worked, it worked!"

The police officer who had found him shook her head. "That's some boy. Did you see all that stuff he had in that bag?" she asked.

"He always has interesting things in his bag, Officer," Lupi said proudly. "He's my brother."

"Come on, buddy." The red-faced officer snapped handcuffs on Hester. "We're charging you with kidnapping and resisting arrest."

"What have I done?" groaned Mark Hester. "Where have all my supporters gone?"

"You've lost them, Mr Hester," the officer replied. "Now they know what you're really like."

We followed the officers outside in time to see the third police officer pushing Nick into the back seat of the police car.

Hester, still fuming, glared at Nick. "You fool!" he cried. "This plan was supposed to secure my success! But now you've ruined me instead."

"Rotten, all of you!" Hester screamed at us as the police placed him, still shouting, next to Nick in the back of the police car.

Drake turned to Tommy, Lupi, and me. "Give me five," he urged, holding out his hand. We laughed and slapped one another's hands.

"Drake, what kind of potion did you give him to make Mark Hester act like that?" Tommy wanted to know.

"It was pretty simple. What he really wanted was a potion that would destroy his opponents, but of course I didn't have anything like that, and even if I did I wouldn't give it to him. So I gave him a potion that would reveal his true character. It wasn't guaranteed to make people vote for him, even though he thought it was."

"But how did the potion work?" I asked.

"It responds to a person's character," Drake explained. "So for a nice person like you, the potion would have shown everyone how good and true you are. But with Hester, the potion let everybody see exactly what he was like underneath all those big smiles."

"He was an animal," Lupi growled.

"I think that's pretty funny coming from you," Tommy teased her, and we all laughed.

"He must be a political animal," said Drake.

I wondered where he'd picked up that expression.

"Do you kids need a ride back to the concert?" a younger officer offered. "You can always come down to the station afterwards and make a full report."

"Sure," we chorused.

The four of us piled into the back seat of another police car. It felt nice to be squashed together again, safe from harm at last!

Chapter 14

"HOPE YOU WIN," the young police officer told us as we climbed out of the police car in front of the concert hall.

"Thanks."

He waved good-bye and we hurried to the entrance.

"I don't know, Sam," Tommy said worriedly. "Look at all the people who are already leaving."

He was right. As we entered the building, the crowd was filtering out into the car park. We hurried to the backstage area.

We spotted Iris and Kimmie standing outside Iris' dressing room. Kimmie was fooling around with the fake fingernails and Iris was stuffing some instruments into a carrier bag. They both looked relieved to see us.

"Lupi, Drake, Samantha!" cried Kimmie, running over and hugging my knees. I hugged her back. "Where did you guys go?"

"It's a long story," I told her. "We'll tell you all about it later."

"Wow, I thought you had disappeared! And right at the most exciting moment!" Iris cried, throwing her arms round us.

"Have they announced the winners yet?" Tommy asked.

"No, you're just in time." She smiled, grabbing my hand. "Let's go and tell them we're back together. The judges were waiting for you to show up before they made their announcement."

Iris seemed so concerned about winning, she didn't ask any more questions about where we'd been for the past two hours. Fortunately there had been lots of contestants, so the concert had lasted a long time.

We checked our appearances in the mirror in Iris' dressing room. Then I picked up Kimmie and we went out to face our audience. The crowd that was filing out of the room looked pleasantly surprised when we came onto the stage. Quickly the audience sat back down and started clapping and whooping.

I glanced over and caught Monica glaring at us from another corner of the stage. Tommy hurried to the front of the stage to tell the announcer that we had all returned.

"The band we've all been waiting for is back with us," shouted the joyful emcee. "After their mysterious disappearance, we welcome Blood back with open arms!" The crowd whooped with excitement.

Goose bumps rose on my arms. I couldn't believe we had generated such enthusiasm. Was this all because of Blood — because people really responded to the way we sounded?

Sure, I knew we were special, but it's somehow different when an audience goes absolutely crazy at the sight of you. No one had ever done that to me before. I figured it must be the Browns — their effect on people. But as I looked at the others — Tommy, Iris, and me — I could see that it was the combination of all of us.

"After much deliberation, the judges have decided upon the winners. We'll start with fourth prize . . . The Winston Binston Band!"

The Winston Binston Band, dressed in fifties' fashion and matching red hightop sneakers, skipped up to the microphone to receive their trophy and a cheque for fifty dollars.

"Third prize goes to . . . The Yellow Jackets!"

Applause followed the group up to the announcer. It seemed like ages since The Yellow Jackets had first introduced us to the Battle of the Bands that time in the mall.

"Our second-prize winners are . . . The Spectaculars!" cried the emcee.

Monica hesitated, as though she couldn't believe what she had heard. Then she glared at me over her shoulder, tossed her feathers, and flounced up to receive her prize. The other members of The Spectaculars seemed ecstatic.

A hush fell over the room as we all waited expectantly for the next announcement.

"Our first-prize winner is the one and only group of its kind — in fact, I don't think we've come up with a category for this band yet. They've introduced some very unusual sounds, and they sure are unusual to look at. I think you'll all agree, this band is something truly special. Congratulations to the winner of this year's Battle of the Bands . . . Blood!"

Chills ran up my arms as a bouquet of blood-red roses was thrust into my arms. I felt like Miss America. All the emotions I'd experienced over the last few hours welled up inside me and made me feel like crying. I didn't, though.

Iris, Kimmie, and Lupi each held identical bouquets of roses. We stood there grinning, breathing the fragrant perfume of the roses. Wow! I thought. At last I've won something.

Iris hugged me. "Can you believe it, Sam? We *won!*"

Flashbulbs started popping all over the room. Iris and I kissed each other, we kissed the Browns, and somewhere in the middle of all this crazy kissing, Tommy and I ended up kissing each other. The touch of his lips on mine spread a warmth all the way through my body. I closed my eyes, wanting to hold on to the moment. I'll always remember his lips pressed against mine — with the sight and scent of those red roses all around us.

"Hey, Sam, you're on TV!" cried my brother Patrick.

It was Monday after school. I sauntered into the living room to see what he was watching. It amazed me to see how comfortable I felt with my new fame. I mean, after being relatively anonymous for most of my life, after one night people had started calling me all the time asking me for my autograph, or just telling me how wonderful our group was. A few days earlier, if my brother had said he saw me on TV, I would have been stunned. It was still exciting, but the possibility of appearing on TV didn't seem all that remote any more.

I guess you'd have to say I was taking it all in my stride.

I peered at the screen, which showed the scene at City Hall, with Mark Hester making a complete fool of himself.

"I just saw you in the middle of City Hall," he said. "I thought you were at the Battle of the Bands on Saturday night. How could you be in two places at once?"

"There you are again — you and Tommy," he cried, pointing at the two of us flanked by the police. "They said you were heroes."

"Well, you can't believe everything you hear," I told him. "Lupi and I are *heroines*."

"I didn't see Lupi in the picture," he noted. "Anyway, they said that these people kidnapped Drake and took him to City Hall. Is that true?"

"Yes, it's true." After our performance, Tommy's parents had driven the four of us to the police department to make a statement. We tried to make our story sound as normal as possible, because we knew the police really didn't believe that Drake could make a politician speak in rhyme or turn him into a raving lunatic. They figured that Hester was crazy to begin with, so it wouldn't take much for a nut like him to decide to kidnap some kids. Drake showed them his current potion, but they just laughed. "It looks like Windrex. You've got some imagination, kid."

After considering this in his usual thoughtful way, Drake offered to give a demonstration. I was glad the police had laughed it off, because for a moment I was afraid Drake would turn the whole police station upside down!

"But why did they kidnap him?" asked Patrick. "What did they want Drake for?"

Before I could think up an answer, our parents came into the room. "Dinner's ready," my father told us.

"Dad, Mum, Sam's on TV," Patrick crowed. "Don't you want to see?"

They hurried over to see me on television, but the City Hall reporter had already finished her story.

"Cloudy skies expected tomorrow and a chance of rain on Wednesday," the announcer said.

"Doesn't look much like our Sam," my dad teased. "But I'm sure we'll see a lot of her on TV from now on."

"Yeah," I said. "Keep those cards and letters coming, fans."

They laughed.

Wednesday afternoon we performed at my school, Davis Junior High. The auditorium was packed for our performance. The whole school and their entire families must've turned up.

We had a reputation for keeping our audience guessing, so we continued to do different and suprising things.

Kimmie had found some ropes attached to the rafters, so while we were signing our "Scare Song", she swung down from the rafters, dressed in bloody rags, and screamed like a banshee, much to the principal's dismay. Mr Owens and some teachers raced up to the stage and circled under Kimmie, urging her to come down.

The crowd clapped wildly as Kimmie landed safely in the middle of the crowd of adults. For our next number, while Lupi and Drake did their funny trancelike dance, we had Kimmie jiggle some skeletons that hung from strings so that the bones clacked together noisily. We had decorated the skeletons with painted-on smiles.

After the performance our fans gathered round to take pictures.

Maurice Maklowitz, equipped with his Polaroid camera, ran over to us. "Hey, Tommy, you know you shouldn't cover this for the school paper because you're in the band," he said excitedly. "So do you mind if I do a story?"

"Sure, go ahead," Tommy answered, grinning for a picture.

Maurice waited for a couple of seconds for his photo to develop. The surface of the photo changed from black to grey, and gradually our images sharpened into focus. Maurice looked troubled.

"You know, for some reason, only you, Tommy, and Iris are showing up, Samantha," he said. "Now, why can't I get a picture of the three Brown kids?"

Randy Alsip came over, looking troubled, too. "I was just about to ask the same question. I can't get a picture of those three, either."

Ms Snell joined the group. "You know, I can't understand it. There may be something wrong with my camera, but the images of the three youngest children haven't turned out at all!"

More and more people repeated their concern about the photographs.

Iris and Tommy examined all the photos carefully and shook their heads.

"Wow, that's really weird," Tommy exclaimed. "Don't you think so, Sam?"

I smiled. "Yes," I said, but I didn't think it was the weirdest thing that had happened lately.

"I guess that means the video won't turn out either," Drake moaned.

I had forgotten all about the video. We hadn't even had a chance to play back the tape yet. If Drake hadn't wanted to make the video so much we would never have got into so much trouble. Money wouldn't have seemed so important to Drake, and he might not have become involved with the kidnappers. It was funny the way things had worked out.

"Maybe it will turn out fine," I tried to reassure him. "But if not, maybe you can come up with a formula to make yourselves appear in photographs."

His eyes lit up. "What a great idea, Samantha! Why didn't I think of that? I'm going to start working on that right away!"

SAMANTHA SLADE

Samantha Slade's an ordinary girl living in an ordinary town; but when she starts a job out of school babysitting for the Brown children, her uneventful life is turned upside down. Because when Dr Brown tells Samantha her children are little monsters, poor Sam doesn't realize that they really *are* monsters! Lupi turns into a werewolf when the moon is full, and Drake sprouts fangs, drinks tomato ketchup by the crateful and concocts the most amazing potions in his laboratory!

Book 1: **Monster-Sitter**
When Samantha Slade agrees to let Lupi and Drake Brown, the two children she babysits, help her with the school Halloween party, she finds she's created the most realistic haunted house ever! Lupi turns into a real werewolf, the fake creepie crawlies become alive, and the whole thing turns into a riot of terrified kids . . .

Book 2: **Confessions of a Teenage Frog**
Samantha Slade should have known better than to accept help from Lupi and Drake when she's campaigning to become class president. Drake makes her a "greatness potion", and before she knows it, she's been turned into a frog! Will Drake be able to turn her back again before she has to make her big speech for the campaign?

Other titles in the SAMANTHA SLADE series:
Book 3   **Our Friend, Public Nuisance No 1**
Book 4   **The Terrors of Rock and Roll**

THE MALL

Six teenagers, all from different backgrounds, with one thing in common – they all want jobs at the new shopping Mall opening in Monk's Way. But working at the Mall brings rather more than most of them had bargained for . . .

Book 1: **Setting Up Shop**

Book 2: **Open for Business**

The new shopping Mall is opening soon, and the six teenagers who work there are already having problems. Ian is fired from his job at Harmony Records because of his dad's interference. Amanda's trying to fend of Mr Grozzi's advances at the restaurant. Jake's trying to hold down two jobs at once. And Simon's temper is threatening to cost him his job at the furniture store. Will life at the Mall prove too tough to handle?.

Look out for the next books in The Mall series:

Book 3: **Gangs, Ghosts and Gypsies**
Book 4: **Money Matters**

You'll find these and many more fun Hippo books at your local bookseller, or you can order them direct. Just send off to *Customer Services, Hippo Books, Westfield Road, Southam, Leamington Spa, Warwickshire CV33 0JH*, not forgetting to enclose a cheque or postal order for the price of the book(s) plus 30p for postage and packing.

HIPPO CHEERLEADERS

Have you met the girls and boys from Tarenton High?
Follow the lives and loves of the six who form the school
Cheerleading team.

CHEERLEADERS NO 19:
MAKING IT Susan Blake £1.50

CHEERLEADERS NO 20:
STARTING OVER Patricia Aks & Lisa
Norby £1.50

CHEERLEADERS NO 21:
PULLING TOGETHER Diane Hoh £1.50

CHEERLEADERS NO 22:
RIVALS Ann E Steinke £1.50

CHEERLEADERS NO 23:
PROVING IT Diane Hoh £1.50

CHEERLEADERS NO 24:
GOING STRONG Carol Ellis £1.50

CHEERLEADERS NO 25:
STEALING SECRETS Anne E Steinke £1.50

You'll find these and many more fun Hippo books at
your local bookseller, or you can order them direct. Just
send off to *Customer Services, Hippo Books, Westfield
Road, Southam, Leamington Spa, Warwickshire CV33
0JH*, not forgetting to enclose a cheque of postal order
for the price of the book(s) plus 30p for postage and
packing.

THE STEPSISTERS
When Paige's Dad marries Virginia Guthrie from Atlanta, she's thrilled that he's found someone to make him happy. But how will she get on with her new stepbrother and stepsisters? Especially Katie, the beautiful blonde fifteen-year-old, who looks like a model and can charm her way out of anything!

1 The War Between the Sisters   £1.75
Not only does Paige have to share her room with her stepsister, Katie, but then she finds that Jake, the boy she's fallen in love with, finds Katie totally irresisitible. Paige's jealousy leads her to do some pretty stupid things to get her own back . . .

2 The Sister Trap   £1.75
Paige is delighted when she gets a job working on the school magazine. Especially when she becomes friendly with the magazine editor, Ben. But her jealousies over her beautiful stepsister, Katie, flare up again when Ben starts taking a lot of interest in Katie's swimming career.

Look out for these new titles in
THE STEPSISTERS series:
3   **Bad Sisters**
4   **Sisters in Charge**

You will find these and many more great Hippo books at your local bookseller, or you can order them direct. Just send off to *Customer Services, Hippo Books, Westfield Road, Southam, Leamington Spa, Warwickshire CV33 0JH*, not forgetting to enclose a cheque or postal order for the price of the book(s) plus 30p per book for postage and packing.

MORGAN SWIFT

Morgan Swift is twenty-four, stunningly beautiful, independent, a great runner, and a fabulous science teacher. And she has the knack of finding trouble – and getting out of it!

MORGAN SWIFT AND THE MINDMASTER

Morgan Swift has an extraordinary ability – she has the power of second sight. And when her mental powers warn her that some of her pupils at Coolidge High are in trouble, she decides to investigate. It's not long before she finds the culprit – a cult leader called Yang who's been giving the kids extra coaching after school . . .

MORGAN SWIFT AND THE TRAIL OF THE JAGUAR

Morgan Swift's two pupils, Jenny Wu and Sally Jackson, are thrilled to be going on holiday with their favourite teacher. And they can't believe their luck when an old friend of Morgan's, the attractive Tom Saunders, invites them to go on an ultra-secret archaeological dig in the South American jungle. But when things start to go wrong, they turn to their teacher to find out exactly what's going on in the jungle . . .

Watch out for more titles in the thrilling MORGAN SWIFT series:

MORGAN SWIFT AND THE LAKE OF DIAMONDS
MORGAN SWIFT AND THE RIDDLE OF THE SPHINX

HIPPO BOOKS FOR OLDER READERS

If you enjoy a really good read, look out for all the
Hippo books that are available right now. You'll find
gripping adventure stories, romance novels, spooky
ghost stories and all sorts of fun fiction to keep you
glued to your book!

HAUNTINGS: Ghost Abbey by Robert Westall £1.95
The Little Vampire in Love
by Angela Sommer-Bodenberg £1.25
Snookered by Michael Hardcastle £1.50
Palace Hill by Peter Corey £1.95
Black Belt by Nicholas Walker £1.75
**STEPSISTERS 1: The War Between the
Sisters** by Tina Oaks £1.75
THE MALL 1: Setting Up Shop
by Carolyn Sloan £1.75
Conrad's War by Andrew Davies £1.75
Cassie Bowen Takes Witch Lessons by Anna
Grossnickle Hines £1.75
Tales for the Midnight Hour by J B Stamper £1.75
Creeps by Tim Schock £1.50

You'll find these and many more fun Hippo books at
your local bookshop, or you can order them direct. Just
send off to *Customer Services, Hippo Books, Westfield
Road, Southam, Leamington Spa, Warwickshire CV33
OJH*, not forgetting to enclose a cheque or postal order
for the price of the book(s) plus 30p per book for postage
and packing.

HIPPO BOOKS FOR YOUNGER READERS

If you've enjoyed this book, you'll probably be
interested to know that there are loads more Hippo
books to suit all kinds of tastes. You'll find scary spooky
books, gripping adventure stories, funny books, and lots
lots more.

You'll find these and many more fun Hippo books at
your local bookshop, or you can order them direct. Just
send off to *Customer Services, Hippo Books, Westfield
Road, Southam, Leamington Spa, Warwickshire CV33
0JH*, not forgetting to enclose a cheque or postal order
for the price of the book(s) plus 30p per book for postage
and packing.

HIPPO CLASSICS

HIPPO CLASSICS is a series of some of the best-loved books for children.

Black Beauty by Anna Sewell £1.50
Black Beauty is a magnificent horse: sweet-tempered, strong and courageous, coloured bright black with one white foot and a white star on his forehead. His adventures during his long and exciting life make one of the most-loved animal stories ever written.

Alice's Adventures in Wonderland
by Lewis Carroll £1.50
When Alice sees the White Rabbit scurry by, her curiosity gets the better of her and she follows him down a rabbit hole. Suddenly she finds herself in an extraordinary world of mad tea parties, grinning Cheshire cats, lobster quadrilles and many more wonderful scenes and characters.

Wind in the Willows by Kenneth Grahame £1.50
One spring day Mole burrows out of the ground and makes his way to the river. There he meets Water Rat and is introduced to all Ratty's friends – Badger, Otter and the loveable and conceited Toad. There's an adventure-filled year ahead for all the animals in this classic story.

Kidnapped by R L Stevenson £1.50
David Balfour is cheated of his rightful estate and then brutally kidnapped. He manages to escape – but is forced to go on the run again when he's wrongfully accused of murder. An action-packed tale of treachery and danger.

The Railway Children by E Nesbit £1.50
The lives of Roberta, Peter and Phyllis are changed completely after the dreadful evening when their father is taken away. They move to the country, where they miss their friends and parties and trips to the zoo. Then they discover the nearby railway, and soon the children find their days filled with adventure.

Heidi by Johanna Spyri   £1.50
An orphan, Heidi is left with her old grandfather who lives high in the mountains. Heidi soon learns to love her life with the kindly old man, the mountains, the goats, Peter the goat boy, and the people of the village. Then one day she is taken away to Frankfurt, and has to leave her friends far behind . . .

The Hound of the Baskervilles
by Arthur Conan Doyle   £1.50
The Baskerville Curse has laid its deadly finger on every member of the family for hundreds of years. When the new heir, Sir Henry, arrives from Canada to claim his inheritance, he asks Sherlock Holmes for his help against the dreadful curse. And with his good friend Dr Watson, Holmes becomes embroiled in one of the most thrilling investigations of his career.

Look out for these titles in the HIPPO CLASSICS series:
A Christmas Carol by Charles Dickens   £1.50
Little Women by Louisa M Alcott   £1.50
White Fang by Jack London   £1.50
Treasure Island by R L Stevenson   £1.50

You'll find all these, and many more Hippo books, at your local bookseller, or you can order them direct. Just send off to *Customer Services, Hippo Books, Westfield Road, Southam, Leamington Spa, Warwickshire CV33 0JH,* not forgetting to enclose a cheque or postal order for the price of the book(s) plus 30p per book for postage and packing.

HIPPO BESTSELLERS

If you enjoyed this book, why not look out for other bestselling Hippo titles. You'll find gripping novels, fun activity books, fascinating non-fiction, crazy humour and sensational poetry books for all ages and tastes.

THE GHOSTBUSTERS STORYBOOK	Anne Digby	£2.50
SNOOKERED	Michael Hardcastle	£1.50
BENJI THE HUNTED	Walt Disney Company	£2.25
NELLIE AND THE DRAGON	Elizabeth Lindsay	£1.75
ALIENS IN THE FAMILY	Margaret Mahy	£1.50
HARRIET AND THE CROCODILES	Martin Waddell	£1.25
MAKE ME A STAR 1: PRIME TIME	Susan Beth Pfeffer	£1.50
THE SPRING BOOK	Troy Alexander	£2.25
SLEUTH!	Sherlock Ransford	£1.50
THE SPOOKTACULAR JOKE BOOK	Theodore Freek	£1.25
ROLAND RAT'S RODENT JOKE BOOK		£1.25
THE LITTLE VAMPIRE	Angela Sommer-Bodenberg	£1.25
POSTMAN PAT AND THE GREENDALE GHOST	John Cunliffe	£1.50
POSTMAN PAT AND THE CHRISTMAS PUDDING	John Cunliffe	£1.50

You'll find these and many more fun Hippo books at your local bookseller, or you can order them direct. Just send off to *Customer Services, Hippo Books, Westfield Road, Southam, Leamington Spa, Warwickshire CV33 OJH*, not forgetting to enclose a cheque or postal order for the price of the book(s) plus 30p per book for postage and packing.